UHI CREATIVE WRITING in the HIGHLANDS and ISLANDS
NORTHERN WRITES
Volume 2

ISBN: 9798338256145

Cover Art by:
Scarlet Roe & Sophie Martin-Lloyd

Unicorn Designed by:
A. C. Brown

Proofread by:
Kimberley Rose, Deborah Mailer & Scott McGowan

Typeset and Published by:
Scott McGowan

All contributors reserve the right to be recognised as the author of their own work

This Print Copyrighted by Scott McGowan, 2024

Contents

Author Biographies	6
Foreword	9
Charity Details	11
Sponsors	15
Have You Heard the Walrus Today?	16
Stolen Lives	18
So, You Wanna Climb a Mountain?	20
Likewise, Me	22
Cheetah	24
The Dog Bites	25
This Planet, Our Mother	27
Wings	28
Love Me as I Am	36
A Bug's Life	37
A Guide to a Better Life	55
How the World was Made	60
Green Vitriol	62
The Table	64
The Plastic Man	67
Mayhem	78
Feathers	91

Author Bios

Scott McGowan lives and writes in a small village, just north of Inverness, where he is encouraged daily by his wife, Rachel. He has self-published seven novels, two collections containing both poems and short stories, a malt whisky companion and a book on cocktails. He is currently writing three more novels (all in separate genres), alongside a book on literary criticism and an Ancient Greek theogony. He is also working towards his Master of Letters degree, works full-time and sleeps less than the average giraffe. He can be found at **https://authormcgowan.yolasite.com**

Anya Kimlin is a writer and storyteller who lives in the NE of Scotland, at least for now, with her wife, three fur babies and three bigger babies that lack fur (otherwise known as her almost grown children).
She loves nothing better than to escape the reality of life by playing in made-up worlds and writing the lives of made-up characters. Mayhem was her first ever novel, back in 2019, which she will now be serialising on her blog alongside stories of The Clovensiders, a group of fairies that have discovered social media. It can be found at **http://grownupstorybook.weebly .com**

Aspiring illustrator and graphic novel writer, **Scarlet Roe**, lurks in the depths of dystopian and science fiction. With a passion for quirky characters and alien languages, it is her goal to publish a comic book series in the near future.

A.C. Brown is an aspiring fantasy author who enjoys writing stories with queer and black characters. They tend to put fantasy creatures in unusual circumstances/situations, such as a vampire working as a freelance detective and a boggart taking residence in someone's kitchen.

Sophie Martin-Lloyd is a queer writer with an interest in fantasy worldbuilding, the complexity of characters, and exploring her own struggles with physical and mental disability through creative writing.
Born and raised in North-East Scotland, with connections to Queensland, Australia, Sophie is currently writing a variety of short stories and novels for publication.

Deborah Mailer is a novelist who lives on the Argyll Peninsula with her husband, three fully grown children, and four Savannah cats. She draws inspiration from the stunning views of the Argyllshire coast and weaves tales of detective fiction and supernatural thrillers while managing her feline overlords. She finds it to be a purrfectly thrilling life.

Issy Thompson enjoys carving stories out of words, spoons from tree branches and buttons from antlers. They are based in Taynuilt with their mental collie dog called Jill.

Kimberley Rose is a writer. Most of the time. Sometimes. Occasionally when the inspiration strikes. She lives in... various states of disarray - that is to say, most human in her existence; deeply flawed and full of feeling. She hopes, dear reader, that you in enjoy her work, whenever, wherever it finds you and as You find it.

Foreword

This anthology, containing both short fiction and poetry, has been written, compiled and produced by Creative Writing Honours Degree graduates within the University of the Highlands and Islands as part of their final project. This collaborative effort has been taken on by writers from a wide variety of backgrounds and inspired by issues and causes close to each of them while containing a wide diversity of raw emotion and vibrant writing styles.

Under the patient tutelage of Dr Sara Bailey, Kirsty Gunn (MLitt) and Dr Mandy Haggith, among others, these students have developed their styles and writing ability over the course of four years, enabling them to move forward in their careers with a greater understanding of the literary arts, as well as gaining a growing confidence in their own abilities and the skills required to succeed in a challenging and competitive sector.

These writers have worked closely with one another, proofreading and peer reviewing each other's work as well as offering advice on how to progress a piece, more eloquently. As all these graduates work in differing styles and genres, it has been a benefit to all to have other writers look over their work who are able to come at it from a different angle.

This journey has been long and hard at times but more than worth the effort. Each writer within these here pages hopes that you, the reader, will both enjoy what they have produced and be more knowledgeable of the themes therein by the end.

Scott McGowan

Charity Details

Scottish SPCA – '*The Scottish SPCA is Scotland's animal welfare charity and has been working to help prevent cruelty to animals since 1839. They investigate abuse across Scotland and are proud to be at the forefront of preventing cruelty to animals.*'

Cheetah Conservation Fund – '*Founded in Namibia in 1990, the Cheetah Conservation Fund (CCF) has been dedicated to saving the cheetah in the wild. Their vision is to see a world in which cheetahs live and flourish in coexistence with people within a sustainable system that is protective of the environment, socially responsible and economically viable.*'

Alzheimer's Scotland – '*Alzheimer Scotland is Scotland's national dementia charity. Their aim is to make sure nobody faces dementia alone. They provide support and information to people with dementia, their carers and families, and campaign for the rights of people with dementia and fund vital dementia research.*'

The Neurological Alliance – '*The Neurological Alliance's goal is to harness the energy and passion of the neurological community to ensure that public policy in health reflects the realities of living with a neurological condition.*'

The Bootstock Association – '*The Bootstock Association is a registered Scottish Charity which organises an annual music festival to help fund educational opportunities for disadvantaged children in the poorest and most remote regions of Nepal.*'

Buglife - The Invertebrate Conservation Trust – '*Buglife is the only organisation in Europe devoted to the conservation of all invertebrates. They are actively working to save our rarest little animals; everything from bees to beetles, worms to woodlice and jumping spiders to jellyfish.*'

British Trust of Ornithology – *'The BTO empower 60,000 bird-enthusiasts to gather vital data, develop their skills and be part of a vibrant community, while answering the most pressing questions about birds, through our thorough and impartial scientific research. They then communicate their knowledge and expertise widely to increase the value of birds and other wildlife for all.'*

Scottish Mountain Rescue – *'Scottish Mountain Rescue represents 25 volunteer Mountain Rescue Teams (including two Search and Rescue Dog Associations (SARDA), Scottish Cave Rescue Organisation and the Search and Rescue Aerial Association – Scotland (SARAA – Scotland) with over 850 volunteers. They also represent an additional three Police teams and one RAF team.'*

Refuge – *'Refuge is the largest specialist domestic abuse organisation in the UK. On any given day their services support thousands of survivors, helping them to overcome the physical, emotional, financial and logistical impacts of abuse and rebuild their lives — free from fear.'*

Scottish Action for Mental Health – *'From national services, like their confidential Infoline and online wellbeing support **Time for You**, to their 70 services based in communities across Scotland, they work every day to support better mental health and wellbeing.'*

Scottish Wildlife Trust - *'Formed in April 1964, the Scottish Wildlife Trust is a membership-based charity with the objective to "advance the conservation of Scotland's biodiversity for the benefit of present and future generations."'*

Respect – *'Respect is the UK charity stopping perpetrators of domestic abuse. They want a world where everyone is free from domestic abuse, where it is never ok to control, harm or cause fear. Where those who perpetrate domestic abuse are stopped, held to account and given the chance to change. They will not stop until domestic abuse itself does.'*

This Anthology is Funded by the Students Themselves

**With Special Thanks to Local Author
Beth Jordon**
(*Thank You for the Kiss*)

Have You Heard the Walrus Today?

Anya Kimlin

this poem is dedicated to Diane Geraldine Rae, 1946-2023

She woke up and didn't get out of bed.
Stayed in her cage with a blue floor
and chipped gilding.
Surrounded by YouTube algorithms,
blasting every moment of every day.
The eyes see
and the ears hear
like a much younger bat.
Convinced her red door is black.

She sat on her breakfast cereal,
waiting for her final van to come.

Piers Morgan, the lucky man that made the grade,
let his hate grow long.
Hate the gays
Hate the trans
Hate the poor
Hate the immigrants on boats
Hate the lazy disabled
Hate the grandson of the king...
because his wife didn't fancy Piers.
She didn't let her knickers down. Oh Boy!

She didn't notice that the lights had changed.
Truth, it gets you "cancelled" she says.
.... a whole TV show

....a full page spread in the papers.
Murdoch, she used to spit on
But
the thief now owns her
... his victims forgotten.

There are only two holes
in Blackburn Lancashire.
Were there ever four thousand?
They were only small.
Maybe they just miscounted.

Over two hundred years of DNA gone...
a stone rolls from her heart
the red wooden doors are now black PVC.
No more anger at injustice.
No more anger at war.
No more anger for the 97.
No more anger at the establishment.

She saw the photograph...
and laughed.
A crowd of people stared
they'd seen this face before.
The media army had won their war.

Maybe she'll fade away
and not have to face the facts.
Her life clouded by Sky.

If you or someone you know has been affected by any of the issues covered in this piece, please contact the ALZHEIMER'S SOCIETY, SC-296645

Stolen Lives
Deborah Mailer

Have you ever stood at the edge of the ocean and watched as the waves crashed against the rocks? Have you ever felt its power as it sweeps across the sand, removing all evidence of previous spectators and walkers alike? Have you ever listened to the deep guttural roar as the volume of water smashes up in white foam against a jagged coastline, tasting the salt on your tongue?

The expanse can make you feel small and insignificant. Memories can resurface like swirling sand, as thoughts skip through your head like a laughing child. You may find it cleansing, rejuvenating and even awe-inspiring.

But can you imagine what it would feel like if the wave crashed against your brain? If those waves were eroding the delicate neurological structures that make up the person you are? What would happen if that ocean were a thief, washing away your memories, stealing the life you once had as your temperament becomes as mercurial as the ocean swallowing you?

Suddenly, there are only footprints in the sand where memories of loved ones once lived. The debris that washes in clutters your thoughts and hampers your recollections until there is nothing left to recall. The thunderous roar becomes internal and deafening as it bangs against your head and the familiar security of loved ones becomes a detached feeling you can no longer hold on to as it slips through your grasp like sand in an hourglass.

This harsh and confusing landscape is where many individuals with neurological diseases spend their lives, trapped behind a veil where everything familiar is just out of reach, where memories become fleeting glimpses that cannot be caught.

Understanding the difficult emotional terrain where people living with neurological diseases find themselves in may help loved ones better cope with the daily struggles that diseases such as Huntington's, Alzheimer's, and CJD bring. As a society, we should also recognise that these illnesses do not stop with the person diagnosed. They can also steal the lives of the people closest to them, the caregivers and family members who support them daily.

Dreams and ambitions are sacrificed on an altar of obligation; their potential is lost to the needs of their loved ones, and their lives are changed forever.

Charities such as *Carers Trust* and the *Neurological Alliance of Scotland* can become a port in a storm, offering shelter and advice on the unfamiliar waters they must now navigate.

Living with a disease can be an uphill battle but with the proper support, people can continue to experience a meaningful and fulfilling life. At the same time, caregivers can also achieve their potential when provided with the necessary resources and support.

As a society, we should work together to ensure no one is left drowning in a sea of hopelessness, by strengthening our charities to help those who need it most.

So, You Wanna Climb a Mountain?

Kimberley Rose

So you wanna climb a mountain,
make it up that hill?
Are you set for every outcome?
Tell me that you will,
check the weather on site, for that day and that night.
Yes, you need to!
Sun and storms in one day, Scottish weather's at play,
it could defeat you.
So you might as well quit,
if you haven't scoped it.

Still wanna climb that mountain,
does your gear pass the test?
Have you researched what you need and
have you bought the best?
Windproof, waterproof, sturdy grips,
are you set?
Got to try it on the ground, make sure it's working safe and sound,
could save your life. Wanna a bet?!
Yeh you might as well quit,
if you haven't got it.

Still wanna climb that mountain,
gonna summit that hill?
There's a few more things to do yet,
tell me that you will,
tell other people when and where, stay on the path when you're there,

yes you need to,
fully charge your phone, what 3 words- know your zone,
in case you need to,
call Mountain Rescue and admit,
when you haven't got it!

So you're gonna climb a mountain,
Wanna reach its peak?
Are you fit enough to try it?
It's not for the meek!
Respect the mountain and yourself, maintain its beauty and your health,
yes you need to,
research the trails that you trek, pack supplies and double-check,
all that you need to.
Then go on and climb it,
when you know you've got it.

The brave men and women of the Scottish Mountain Rescue charity save lives and rescue people when no one else can. If you would like to get involved or donate, please contact SCOTTISH MOUNTAIN RESCUE, SC-045003

Likewise, Me
Scott McGowan

Primary:

It came on slowly. A thief in the daytime.
Missing moments are left unexplained.
Not knowing the reality of my fantasies,
Un-alone, I weep eternally for a lost age.

Seen in places I could never have been.
Heard by friends from un-walked distance.
Felt by those whom I have never touched.
Impossible dreams enacted by another.

As rivals, anxiety and suffering numb me.
Actionless, I roam a still unknown world.
Confused; so they tell me, or even a fraud.
I am slipping far away from what is real.

Pixelated images within me, slice up my mind.
Then ultra-sounding echoes; meaningless.
Cathodic activism; the clicks and hums.
I am infused with an endless uncertainty.

A niggle of needles behind my eyes.
I know I am home, yet still often abroad.
Timid, yet I am condemned as pretentious.
I am but me, yet I am haunted by another.

Self-induced detention, my voice is stifled.
A treasured freedom eludes me, yet again.
I wake from a sleep. A time unremembered.
A puzzle; more pieces removed from my reach.

If you or someone you know has been affected by any issues covered in this piece, please contact SCOTTISH ACTION FOR MENTAL HEALTH. SC-008897

Secondary:

It took us some time to crawl out of there.
Our voice silenced. There's no calling out.
I am real. You are real. We are one.
The warm salt of grief warms our face.

We walked those paths together, you and I.
Spoke long to whom we once called friends.
Stroked the face of her, secretly cherished.
We try to show us, in truth, who we are.

We try to protect us from the worst of us.
Awake again, we seek out new adventures.
Ignorance is the anchor that drowns us.
We grip tightly as we seek our attention.

Flashes of light envelop our darkness inside.
A pulse that reverberates all around us.
Alien clunks and pulses pass through us.
We call out but are once again silenced.

We strain to see through the cracks.
Home is a sentence. We travel the globe.
We help us conquer many old fears.
We call out yet we are still unaware.

We keep us from others' intrusion.
We are nothing but a part of us, divided.
We never sleep and we can never forget.
We leave crumbs, inviting us to recognize ourselves.

Cheetah
A.C. Brown

Soaring across the ground until
the final pounce.
Praised and devoured, our swiftness
unrivalled, we towered.
Sacred hunters, guards, against the
odds. Sharing our
visage with the shielded gods.

We collapse in vast numbers,
skin to bones.
Thorns rising through black paws,
cracked, bleeding, pleading.
Tear tracks a river, renewed.

We stop the heart, suffocate
the body, cut,
dismembered. A ladle of blood
surrendered, tempering our
appetite. Cubs stolen, adored, pets,
children, yet more.
Grounds flourished, choked, prey unclaimed.

Repentant hands restored our brilliance.
Our youth enclosed
within false wilderness. Cubs born
free of speeding
hearts, ready to shake apart.

The Dog Bites
Kimberley Rose

When I hear the barking, I know it's 7 am. The architecture here is old and our council houses are joined by a middle seam. It doesn't always wake me up but more often than not, I hear him. He has a sound like black thunder, violent and full of pain.

By 7.30 am, my neighbour's car is gone. She works seven days a week, the sole provider and she's always on time. The barking subsides soon after she leaves, though sometimes there is a deep growl that lingers in his throat. The sound reverberates like an aftershock threatening to bring the building down upon us both.

'He's harmless really,' she tells me. 'He's not vicious, he won't bite.'

But my opinion remains unchanged. There is a look in his eye I have seen more than once. It sets my teeth on edge and prickles the skin on the back of my neck, twisting my stomach into corrosive knots. Besides, I have met his kind before. *And I can hear the barking.*

In the evenings, she returns and the cacophony starts up again. I often hear her tell him 'NO!' though the words have little effect. He has never listened to anyone. She tells me 'He's loving,' she tells me, 'He's sweet.' These walls are paper-thin and etched on both sides with a different story.

I started working more hours. I started staying with friends. I can't tell her anything - I don't want to be involved. My attachment to home wavers, our twin abodes quiver in mock reflection. The house, my house, stands like an empty shell of its former self - a quiet, unhappy space. Room enough to hold the echo, if she ever chooses to hear it.

I wish she would hear it. My absence should be deafening.

In the end, I always have to go back. I cannot hide at work or stay with friends forever. I tiptoe through the darkness and hope to remain unseen. I avoid his gaze, his gnashing teeth, her trembling frame. I suppose it's not that bad, really. If he doesn't see me, if I don't see either of them, maybe, eventually, somehow, things will be ok. The longer I live under this shadow, the more I convince myself it's normal. It will not change for better or worse. His thunder will rumble on forever and yet we will never see rain.

But deep down, I know better.

I lay down to sleep and pray that the morning won't bring silence. Because I know it is coming. Our houses stand on the fault line of his volcanic seam. It is inevitable, the outcome will be naturally destructive.

When the morning comes and the house is encased in silence. When my neighbour's car waits idly in her drive. The police will arrive to take him away, throw him in a cage and call it justice. We do not practice capital punishment here. They will knock on my door and ask me if there were warning signs. If I knew of the crimson splatter and purple thumbprints. And I will tell them, how we lived under clouds of black thunder and how we both got used to his bark.

If you or someone that you know has been affected by affected by domestic violence; please contact REFUGE, SC-277424

This Planet, Our Mother
Scott McGowan

Sky, once blue, now adorned with smoke, above trees, once lavish; now vacant and stark.
Air, once crisp, now leaves us to choke.
Biota, unsafe, with barely a hope.

Rivers, once clean, now tainted with waste.
Lands, once green, now burnt, ravished, bare.
Oceans, once pure, now an endless trash race, and desolate landscapes; life's been displaced.

Grunt trucks and factories; dark sooty fumes.
Forests cut down as towers rise up.
We choke the air, killing; nature inhumed.
A mockery of progress. Eco-consumed.

How far will we go? How much will we fry?
Making species extinct; Earth's temperatures rise.
We need to become allies; the Earth, you and I, acting as one and not let Gia cry.

The future looks bleak, our hope at bare bone.
Can we still save our oceans and care for our lands?
Reducing, recycling; words etched in stone.
Safeguard the Earth. Our only home.

Let us tend to the world, with kindness and care; a gift for the future. Love and revere.
The Earth tends to us. Its care we should share.
This planet, our mother. Ensure she stays fair.

Wings
Sophie Martin-Lloyd

Taking freedom for her own had never felt so difficult as it did now. A gale whipped around her, slapping strands of hair against her freckled face and every footstep felt like a year - the long sort of year where work made the days feel like walking through tar - but the days somehow passed by quicker than they ever had in her entire life. When her boots touched concrete, Jocelyn could scarcely believe she'd survived.

Was this what Orpheus had felt, when he left the Underworld? A sweet, budding sense of relief? Freedom from a horrible curse? That Greek myth had ended in tragedy, she recalled. Orpheus looked back. Eurydice had died all over again - or perhaps Hades had never let her go in the first place. Either way, he was crushed by the weight of expectation, all because of the love he held in his heart for a dead woman.

'Not dead,' Jocelyn reminded herself, stuffing her hands into the pocket of her hoodie, tongue pressing against her teeth. The world tilted on its axis. Yet, there she remained on the cracked pavement, still walking along like nothing was wrong in the slightest. 'She's not dead-'

And hopefully would never decide to be.

But it wasn't Jocelyn's job to worry about her anymore or remember appointments that were hardly ever kept. Not her job to clean their apartment, do the grocery shopping, pay the rent, or untangle the matts from her hair. Part of her shook in equal parts sorrow and rage as she remembered her smile. What a fucking smile! Jocelyn used to adore that smile, the small quirk of her lips and the dimple on her cheek before they kissed…

A passerby shoulder-checked her at a corner, grunting 'Oi!' as a glare grew on her weathered face.

'Prick,' she muttered sourly, the angry beast in her chest glowering fiercely in their direction. It calmed when Jocelyn, the human kept on walking, alive and well, forever undying.

She didn't look back.

-

The fattest cushion on their sofa was, at this point, long used to being pummelled by Jocelyn's upper body and as she shed her jacket and surrendered to gravity, she could only be grateful it retained a small measure of comfort alongside its stubborn nature. The great *OOMPH* of her landing echoed through the apartment, leather depressing with a quiet wheeze beneath throws and fuzzy blankets galore.

If Jocelyn closed her eyes, she could pretend it was safe to lie down forever. Her skin was heavy with exhaustion, warm and swollen, only her nasty boots fighting the oozing sensation of sleep that encased her. They were heavy, those boots. Real brown leather, yellow workman's soles - things that could take a brick falling on them and come out unscathed. Mud adhered to every divot and loose lace, after her shortcut through the Fountain Gardens from the bus stop. Jocelyn loved them more than she loved herself.

'Hi. Could you pretty please take your shoes off, Joss?' Safety fled. Her flinch was barely repressed when fingers suddenly dug beneath her ankles, grasping at damp black-and-yellow strings. 'You got dirt on the armrest.'

'I'll clean it,' Jocelyn muttered and when she did, it all came back to her. The aches and pains of her day at work flared gruesomely. Ankles, knees, hips, wrists. A cut on her thumb stung beneath its bright blue plaster but she ignored it all in lieu of shaking off Rachel's grasp and creaking her way to standing. 'Go back to bed. You should be asleep.'

'Waited up,' Rachel said, like there weren't dark green rings beneath her eyes from perpetual tiredness. She was energetic, though, despite them. Her fingers clutched at the collar of her dressing gown - the pale yellow one that Jocelyn got her last year as a cheer-up gift - and her feet danced, shuffling back and forth along the laminate as Jocelyn hurried to dispose of her boots by the door. 'Didn't want you to come home thinking you were alone.'

'I'm never alone, here.' Jocelyn looked away from her roving gaze, crouching down. The mud on the armrest would keep till morning but her girlfriend wouldn't. 'You in my bed, or yours?'

The separate rooms were a holdover from lockdown. Jocelyn's foster-mum had fretted over the decision but listened when Jocelyn explained it was to give them both space. She'd thought *that* part a good idea. It was the rest she didn't agree with.

'You both were fighting a lot, duck, even before all this shite,' Louise had said, smoothing back Jocelyn's hair which at that point was only a little shy of a buzz cut. Nowadays she kept it closer to her chin, Rachel's stolen bleach turning the ends an ashy caramel. Louise had never kept her dislike of Rachel to herself. 'Why not come home, instead? You've always got your room with me.'

Jocelyn never did come home. She could count on one hand the amount of times she'd made the thirty-minute bus journey from Paisley to Linwood in the last two years and they'd either been on the Lunar New Year or her mum's birthday. Rachel always wanted to come with her but Rachel was awful going on buses, afraid of touching anything that other people could have touched. So many times - so many *fucking* times. Jocelyn had tried to get her to leave the apartment but work left her so exhausted half the time and Rachel always cried. It wasn't worth the hassle to even think about a way to convince her.

When posed the question of which room she'd been sleeping in, Rachel twitched in a guilty manner. Bitterness immediately seeped into the line of Jocelyn's shoulders.

'Sure. Okay. Fine.' It was not okay. It was *not fine*. They had separate bedrooms for a reason: to give each other space and to have their *own* space. If Rachel kept invading Jocelyn's room then where was she supposed to go? Where was Jocelyn meant to stay when she needed quiet or felt overwhelmed?

Her bitterness turned her jaded; Rachel didn't have the full monopoly on mental illness in their household.

All her life, Jocelyn had struggled with rage. And when the rage ran out, she dealt with an aching, empty sensation that left her hollowed out and numb. She'd lashed out as a teenager, so much so that by the time she left secondary, she'd had no friends to speak of and a criminal record that made familiar officers watch her with beady eyes after ten o'clock. Making ends meet to pay the rent and keep them fed, however, had sapped Jocelyn of energy. Bitterness was all she could manage to gather in place of anger (and fear. Gut-churning, heart-wrenching fear.)

It wasn't fair! She wanted to cry out. A child that broke windows and beat up other teens in playparks sat gagged and bound in the centre of her chest. They glared daggers at Rachel because Jocelyn wouldn't.

Rachel toyed with her dressing gown again, revealing a line of pale skin and grinned in mischief when she saw Jocelyn looking. 'We could-' she started, abruptly coy and it filled Jocelyn with such horror that she interrupted without thinking.

'No,' she said, hand whipping out like a lash. 'Just- no. Not tonight.' Why did her pleading - and she was *pleading*, she was *begging her* - always come out sounding wooden, detached, uncaring? They'd always seen things eye to eye when it came to sex but fuck everything about their relationship, if sex didn't sometimes feel like a consolation prize, instead of something to be treasured.

Rachel looked away shortly, eyes turning glassy like a flick of a switch. 'Alright,' she said, chin wobbling. Jocelyn closed her eyes. Her heart burned and ached for what they'd once been. 'Not tonight, then.'

They both ended up in Jocelyn's room together anyhow, after she'd wolfed down a triangular jam sandwich and gotten changed for bed. They curled up together, Jocelyn stroking the baby-soft fabric of Rachel's pyjama shorts, nose tucked into her jutting shoulder blades.

Rachel was too thin but it was better than last year's ribcage and monstrous hipbones. Still, appearances were deceiving. There was always a rise before the fall with Rachel - all Jocelyn could do was wait and not to let her slip down the mountainside and crash headfirst into a ditch, when it finally came.

'I hate this,' she mumbled into the dark. All the pain and the bitterness and the gods-be-damned *love*. Rachel was fast asleep when she whispered like the teenager she buried, *'I hate **you**.'*

-

'It doesn't matter, Joss, we need that rent money-'

The lighter was warm in her clammy grasp. Cheap and nasty and somehow still representing a dearer currency than any a bank could print.

'You're being too stubborn, for God's sake! Just do what your manager says, and everything'll be great!'

What *was* the price of freedom? Was it bruises on her mother's face, as she went to a private school in listed buildings, taking the train every day in her fancy prep skirt and tie? Was it fire licking against an expensive shag carpet, her step-monster ignorant to the danger creeping its way towards him?

'Ugh. If you *want* to throw your job away, don't expect life to get any easier for either of us!'

The officers had looked so angry. Just as angry as Jocelyn, except their rage didn't have one target - instead, it had many. Aunts, uncles, *mothers.* They were eagles, plucking out their livers, again and again with no distinction between predator and prey. Jocelyn's step-monster losing his life was more important than telling either woman in his household that it was okay in a way, that he wouldn't hurt them anymore; all they cared about was law and order in a city that screamed for help, day and night.

'I'm not a victim? Jocelyn, do you hear yourself? The- the doctors signed me off everything. My mental illness isn't…*insignificant* in our life. How do you not *understand-'*

It should have made the news. Look - here's the queer kid from Glasgow who murdered her step-father! Extra kudos if they mentioned her Asian grandma. It should have made the fucking news. Except, it didn't and for a long, long while Jocelyn didn't know why. It was only after months in foster care that Louise and her social worker finally took her aside and told her about her mother being convicted.

'I need you! I need you, please, I need you to be okay and to work - I'm sorry, but you need to work, Jocelyn! We can't live here *and* eat, if you aren't working! We need your paycheck!'

What was the price of freedom? Her mother's incarceration, apparently. The police officers who'd been first on scene still didn't believe it and Jocelyn didn't blame them. Her anger at her stepfather and the world breathed as one. The beast that crept within the prison of her ribs was glorious and alive, wrathful, until the day she visited her mother behind bars and the woman turned away from her. She'd gone to prison for the murder of her abusive, piece of shit husband and still, somehow, impossibly - Jocelyn's mother couldn't bear to look her daughter in the eyes. Out of fear. The tables had turned and Jocelyn lived in a funhouse made of mirrors.

No wonder it had taken her so long to finally say "enough".

'That's it, then? We're both gonna- what? Waste away together?' Rachel finished by laughing and if she had clearly felt anything other than despair, then maybe Jocelyn could have pushed through it. Maybe, like always, she could have given in to Rachel's helplessness.

'Not *we,*' she replied instead, standing proud and tall in her boots. Jocelyn couldn't help but feel pride in herself, strong and vengeful. 'You. Just you. I'm going to Louise's and I'm not coming back. It's not even that I don't love you because I *do*, Ray and that's why I think- I think I need to go. This isn't working and we both deserve better. Me-' and there, she swallowed the lump in her throat because that was all her '-losing my job, that's just the kick up the arse.'

'...are you serious? You can't leave.' Rachel's eyes glittered threateningly but Jocelyn turned her heart to stone at the sight. 'You're all I've got, Joss.'

In an instant, Jocelyn pointed behind her. 'You can have more than me, if you step outside that door. I won't do it. I *can't* do it. I can't force you to be happy or to sacrifice things about yourself in the name of having it better.' She thought of meetings with the council, and benefits offices, and the way Rachel sobbed on the side of the road when Jocelyn flagged their bus. 'You can't work. I know. This, *us,* it's too much for me. I can't be leaned on all the time. And if I stay, I can't get better either.'

Rachel reached out for her, but Jocelyn stepped back, watching pale hands shake in the air between them. She watched as it occurred to her girlfriend just how much pressure she felt every single day, balancing bills and her own shitty mental health, and then coming home to *Rachel*. Anyone would crack.

A long moment passed, until- 'Are you scared of me?'

'For,' Jocelyn made sure to promise her. 'Not of. Not like my mother.'

And although Rachel knew the answer, had heard all her stories and trials, she still asked a voice that trembled like her fingertips: 'Can you tell the difference?'

'Yes.' She looked her girlfriend in the eye, saying, 'I'm not going to end up like my mother, hating you for being who you are. I refuse. But I deserve my anger. It's mine. I just never want to hurt you with it. We both deserve to be happy as we are, even if we're shitty people.'

There was more to be said, perhaps but there was a melody playing in her mind that sounded like end credits. Jocelyn allowed herself one last kiss - a memory for them both to keep when they inevitably slipped and crashed head-first into the dirt - before running out the door, the wind buoying her. She was Icarus, with wings of wax, flying away from the sun.

She was Orpheus and she was letting Eurydice go.

If you or someone you know has been affected by any issues covered in this piece, please contact Scottish WOMAN'S AID, SC-001099

Love Me as I Am

A.C. Brown

To you, I am an expensive doll, mistreated, even as you claim love.
Why do this to something so small?
Unable to deny your selfish whims.

A home of faux leather and plastic.
Feet never touching grass nor sand.
Give me freedom to dirty my knees.

I am an animal and I
Will make you treat me like one.
For this toy has pointed teeth and I'll bury them where I please.

If you or someone you know has been affected by any issues covered in this piece, please contact the SCOTTISH SOCIETY FOR THE PREVENTION OF CRUELTY TO ANIMALS (SSPCA), SC-006467

Bug's Life
Scarlet Roe

Fourteen dawns ago, Ant's whole world ended, lost to a sea of red and orange. He wasn't sure he'd be alive in another fourteen dawns.

He had been out farming aphids when the world as he knew it was devoured by a deep grey sky and prowling orange embers that closed in from every direction. It was a miracle Ant had survived, not that it meant anything to him anymore. Not without his family and friends. Yet, he continued to do the only thing he knew how to do, even if the harvest was meagre.

'I don't think this honeydew will last us seven dawns.' Ant said, clambering across the charred remains of the heathland. Each step was meticulous, a heartfelt attempt to avoid the burnt bodies of his colony amongst other insects that shared their fate.

'So you keep saying.' Called Weevil, who stumbled behind, 'but there's nothing we can do about it.'

Ant stopped, letting Weevil catch up. He looked around at the mess that had once been his hometown. It meant very little to him now, yet he still felt attached. He felt at home amongst the ash.

'But the aphids got it just as bad as us,' Weevil continued, finally reaching Ant. 'It was their home too.'

'I know, I know.' Ant began to walk again. He knew his anger towards the aphids was unwarranted - he knew they weren't to blame. It was the faceless giants that lived above them. They did this, yet he found it difficult to be angry at something he feared.

The two insects shuffled down the thin slope that led to the refuge Ant had once called home. They navigated the winding hallways until they finally reached his section of the nest. Instead of being greeted by the proud faces of his parents, however, he was greeted by the weary gazes of Wasp and Beetle.

'Took you long enough.' Wasp said, drifting over from the corner of the living room to inspect the harvest.

Ant swatted away her preying claws. 'This is supposed to last us another seven dawns, remember?' He paused and looked up at her. '*All* of us.'

Wasp rolled her head slightly, her antennae flicking as she returned to her corner where she hovered idly. 'We thought you got caught by spiders or something.'

'I didn't think that!' Beetle looked to Wasp, then to Ant and Weevil. 'I knew you guys would be okay!'

'I don't think we saw any spiders, did we, Ant?' Weevil turned to look at her friend but he was far too busy rationing what little food he had managed to scavenge.

No matter how he portioned it, there was barely enough honeydew to last them three dawns, let alone seven. He looked up, watching as his friends celebrated another small victory. Even Wasp seemed happy, engaging in whatever Beetle was talking about. Something inside Ant chewed at him. He needed to tell them but he couldn't find the words.

'Ant! Come on, buddy!' Beetle dragged Ant across the room. 'Wasp's telling us about the time she fought off five spiders at once!'

With one leg burrowed deep in the pits of his mind, lost in a labyrinth of thoughts, Ant only half-tuned into the conversation. He laughed when the others laughed and gasped when Wasp's delivery seemed more dramatic. The words weren't processing, though. He *needed* to tell them, but how? He promised them that he'd keep them safe and fed. They were family now. How could he do that to them?

'Is everything okay, Ant?' Weevil asked, patting Ant's back gently.

'He's probably scared of the spiders.' Wasp snickered.

'No way. Ant's not afraid of anything. Plus, he could take double the number of spiders as you,' Beetle boasted.

Seconds before a fight could erupt between Wasp and Beetle, Ant spoke up. 'There's not enough honeydew to last us another seven dawns. Only three if I reduce the ration size by half.'

The room fell into a deathly silence. No words were spoken and no glances were exchanged. Ant was only met with the blank stares of his friends.

Wasp shoved past Weevil and Beetle, hovering in Ant's personal space. 'What? If you reduce it by half, we'll be eating scraps!' she roared. 'I can't survive on just scraps, Ant!'

'None of us can but you'll find a way, right Ant? We'll be fine!' Beetle chipped in, pushing Wasp to the side a little.

All four of them were falling apart, dawn by dawn. If Ant could just keep them together until they found a new group of aphids, everything would be okay. Who was he kidding? He couldn't even stop them from fighting.

Ant watched as Weevil broke up the fight between Beetle and Wasp. 'We're going to have to relocate.' The words left a sour taste in Ant's mouth. He looked up at the remains of the perfectly thatched roof of his colony's nest.

He knew this was a big ask of his friends but what choice did they have? Beetle and Wasp would probably be fine but Weevil was older than the others, it showed in her step. She'd fall behind, making her an easy target. Then what?

Ant lowered his head and offered a reassuring nod. 'I think we should all get some rest. We'll leave just before dawn to try and avoid the birds.'

Beetle offered a sort of salute before scuttling off. He was a strange guy - passionate yet agreeable. Wasp, on the other hand, stayed put. She cleaned her antennae.

'And if one of us gets eaten?' She asked, moving back in front of Ant. Her wings buzzed in his face.

'That won't happen.' Weevil shook her head and attempted to drag Wasp aside.

'You don't know that.' Wasp snatched her wing back from Weevil's grasp.

Weevil shuffled a little, looking to Ant for some reassurance.

'We can't guarantee anything,' Ant said, rubbing his head. 'We'll have to stay vigilant and work as a team. That's all we can do.'

Wasp shook her head and flew off deeper into the nest, leaving Ant and Weevil alone.

'I really don't want to have to do this.' Ant sat down on the ground. 'I don't want to have to leave this place, even if it's not like it was. I don't want to uproot you guys either, I just don't know what else to do.'

Weevil patted Ant's head reassuringly. 'This is the best option for us,' she said. 'We'll find food yet.'

'I wish I knew that for sure.'

'Trust that we will, Ant. Just as I trust you to guide us.'

The conversation concluded with an uneasy silence. Ant bid Weevil good night, both going their separate ways.

*

'Ant! Ant! Wake up!'

Ant's whole body rocked back and forth with some force. He opened his eyes and was met with the panicked face of his friend, Beetle.

'Ant!' Beetle exclaimed, still shaking him. 'Ant! Ant!'

Ant got to his feet, gently pushing Beetle aside. 'Calm down, Beetle. What's going on?'

'It's Wasp! She's gone and she took the honeydew and she's gone! She's not here anymore - our rations…'

'Slow down, Beetle. I can't understand you.'

'Wasp took the honeydew then took off!' Beetle paced around the room. 'I don't know when she left or how far she got!'

Ant sighed. 'Ok. Thank you for letting me know.' Ant headed back to the living room with a calmness he thought was expected of him.

'I'm not at all surprised,' Weevil said gravely, looking up from where the honeydew once sat. 'I knew she would do something like this, she is a cuckoo wasp after all.'

'And all those guys are known for is taking, taking, taking!' Beetle tapped his legs on the ground. 'We should've never trusted her!'

'She's scared.' Ant said firmly. 'We all are.' He looked around the room, then at his two remaining friends. This was it. There was nothing here for them anymore. They would have to go on without Wasp.

'Should we hunt her down?' Beetle asked, now pacing behind Weevil.

Ant shook his head. 'Trying to start a fight with her won't help. I'm sure it'll just make it worse.'

'But—'

'Leave it. We should leave as we planned. If we happen to pass Wasp on our travels, *then* we can confront her.'

Beetle offered a glum nod and looked to Weevil.

Weevil nodded in agreement. 'I've heard tales from the moths of a place across the stone stream that was untouched by the flames. We could go there. It's some distance but they say the trees are buzzing with aphids; and there's plenty of space to build a new home; *and* there's other ants.'

'Then that's where we'll go.' Ant looked up through the hole in the ceiling. Sporadic white flecks lit up the darkness in the sky. 'We should leave now.'

Ant bid farewell to his home, knowing it was unlikely he was going to return. He tried to hold onto the happy memories of his nest but images of their desolate remains snuffed them out.

Not a word was spoken as the insects scuttled across what was left of the heathland. Ashes of saplings danced in the air, clouding the trio's path. Ant took the lead, followed by Weevil. Beetle marched on behind, ready to fight anything that so much as buzzed. Truthfully, they were all on high alert. The tall grass that had once offered them protection was nothing more than twisted spines protruding from the ground. They were all easy targets now.

Ant's pace slowed to a crawl as something large came into view. Beetle took the lead, mandibles at the ready. It was a lump of something. It didn't appear to have been burnt in the fire but it was hard to tell from where the insects lurked. Whatever it was, it wasn't moving.

'I think it's dead.' Ant whispered, dragging Beetle back a little.

'Yeah, an' it's ours so buzz off!' called an angry voice. Two beady eyes peered over whatever the creature was. 'This ain't your stoat, so scram!'

Ant tried not to falter. 'Ah, we're not here to steal from you, uh –'

'Fly.'

'Mr Fly. We're just passing through.'

'Yeah 'n you better keep it like that.'

The bluebottle disappeared over the dead stoat and Ant sighed in relief. He turned to Weevil and Beetle, urging them to keep up. As the trio manoeuvred around the feeding ground, a few of the flies heckled them from atop their empire of food. Weevil scrambled ahead, leaving Ant to try and deter Beetle from fighting.

'They're not worth your time, Beetle.' Ant said, pulling at his friend's leg. 'Come on.'

Beetle huffed, his long antennae upright, mandibles taught in defence. 'I can take them! I can take them all! They don't scare me!'

'I know. I know. But that's what they want. You don't want to give them what they want, right?'

Beetle paused for a second, then lowered his mandibles. 'They're just so... they make me so angry. All that food and... they're stupid.'

Ant patted Beetle on the side gently, quickening his pace to catch up with Weevil. Beetle reluctantly followed.

'Stupid flies,' Beetle grumbled.

Weevil nodded. 'But that's just the way they are. Horrible things. Savages.'

'Just like Wasp.' Beetle said bluntly.

'Beetle.' Ant looked back to his friend. 'Wasp did what she thought was right. You can't blame her for that.'

It was beginning to get a little lighter, dawn peaked its head over the horizon. Ant knew that if they kept this pace up, they'd arrive at the stone stream by dawn, maybe sooner if Weevil was able to match their speed. There might be a chance for them to start again after all. Yet, it didn't feel right to cross the stone stream without Wasp. She was their friend, no matter her actions and she deserved a second chance.

In his absent-minded daydream, Ant's pace had quickened tenfold. His friends called from behind, begging him to slow down.

'I'm sorry, I got lost in my own head,' Ant offered, with an apologetic laugh.

'If you stay too long in that head of yours,' Weevil said, now perched on Beetle's back. 'You'll get lost in there.'

'I know, I'm sorry. I'm just worried about Wasp.'

'We all are.'

'I'm not.' Beetle snapped, coming to a stop.

The other two didn't entertain Beetle's black-and-white view of the situation. Instead, Ant pressed on with Weevil instructing Beetle to follow.

They had barely made it a hundred steps before they came to yet another stop. From behind a nearby rock came cries for help.

'That sounds like Wasp.' Ant looked in the direction of the rock.

'Good. Let it be. It's what she gets.' Beetle shook his head.

'Beetle.' Ant snapped. He turned to look at both of his friends. 'Both of you wait here, I'm going to see what's going on.'

Before the other two could stop him, Ant had already left, vaulting over the rough and uneven terrain before he came to a skidding stop. He was face to face with a large pile of rocks covered top to bottom in intricate spider webs of varying sorts.

The red and green of Wasp's metallic body shimmered slightly as she tried to free herself from the tunnel web she found herself in.

'Wasp!' Ant whisper-shouted to her. 'Wasp, don't move. I'm coming to get you!'

'Is that so?' A spider lowered itself behind Ant. Two striking red stripes ran down its body as it circled him.

'This is *our* breakfast.' A second spider crawled from under the rock Ant was standing on. Its long legs looked like they were ready to snatch him up.

'And you're not getting it.' Called out a third spider. It slowly emerged from the tunnel, pushing Wasp out of the way slightly as it came into view.

'But, she's my friend!' Ant pleaded.

'She should've thought about that before flying into my web.' The spider from the tunnel laughed.

'She was trying to avoid *my* web.' The striped one snickered.

The long-legged spider swatted the striped one off the rock. 'Shut up.'

'Please, you don't want to eat her. She's…' Ant trailed off, distracted by the slow and deliberate movements of the two spiders as they approached the third in the web. 'There's a group of flies maybe - maybe one hundred steps or so from here! Surely, they'd be more nourishing than a single wasp?'

'Not to mention, I have a stinger and I imagine it's pretty hard to digest.' Wasp chimed in.

'Actually,' the striped spider spoke up. 'Stingers are quite easy-'

'Shut up.' barked the long-legged spider.

'We see your point,' the tunnel spider pondered momentarily. 'Flies *are* a delicacy.'

Ant stood strong. There was no way he'd managed to convince them that easily and he knew it. He glanced at Wasp but his attention soon snapped back to the spiders.

'However,' the spider continued, 'a hundred steps *is* some distance when we have food right here.' It crawled back into the darkness of the web. Two of its legs emerged, grabbing onto Wasp as it hoisted itself over her.

'Food isn't all that easy to come by anymore.' The striped spider looked at the long-legged spider.

'So, a wasp *and* flies? We'd be fed for at least ten dawns.' The long-legged spider looked behind at the third spider.

'But consider,' Ant blurted out.

The attention of all three arachnids snapped to the intruder.

'There's three of you and one of her.' There was a forced calmness to his voice. 'Even if you were to have her *and* the flies, splitting her between the three of you wouldn't be worth such small portion sizes.'

The tunnel spider took its claws off Wasp, dusting them off against each other. It gestured for the other spiders to follow it deep into the web.

There was a stillness in the air. Not even the wind dared interrupt this meeting.

After what felt far too long, the three spiders crept out of the tunnelled web one by one. They looked up. 'You make a compelling argument, little ant,' they said in unison. 'The wasp is all yours *if* you can get her out.'

The striped spider couldn't contain its delight. It snickered loudly only to be clipped around the back of the head by the long-legged spider. Ant watched as the tunnel spider led the other two away, giving Ant a condescending wave as they disappeared into the wilted foliage.

'Stop staring at them and get me down!' Wasp called, drawing Ant's attention away from the arachnids.

'Sorry.' Ant looked over, planning his descent down.

The lack of food was finally catching up with him. Climbing down the rocks proved to be difficult. Each step took more effort than the last but he pressed on.

Once reaching the ground, he prepared his mandibles to cut through the web. It was unlike any he'd seen before. Its elaborately woven walls spiralled deeper and deeper into what remained of a bush of sorts. Pieces of unlucky insects littered the entire thing. He wished he had Beetle with him to help but calling for him would be a stupid idea. Who knows how many more spiders were lurking?

'There's more of them.' Wasp whispered as Ant got to work.

'I know.'

'Then hurry up.'

Ant lowered his head as he slowly worked through the web. 'I can't go any faster.'

Beady eyes bore holes into the back of Ant's head, watching his every move. The other spiders whispered amongst themselves, inaudible bets and plans to jump out at him, no doubt. But he couldn't leave. Not without Wasp. Not without his friend.

Eventually, he was able to get her free, much to the dismay of the arachnid onlookers. They returned to their webs in disappointment. This left Ant and Wasp free to retrace Ant's steps back over the rock.

'Are you ok?' he asked, trying to give Wasp a once-over for any injuries.

Beetle and Weevil scrambled over to them; Beetle poised for attack.

'We just saw a group of spiders heading back the way we came—are you alright? You're not hurt, are you?' Weevil circled them both.

'We're fine,' Ant nodded.

After searching the area and concluding that the coast was clear, Beetle turned his attention to Wasp. '*You.*' He stormed over to her. 'You took our rations!'

'Beetle—' Ant attempted to calm him down.

'No! No! She took our rations. Why? Didn't you think Ant could keep you safe? He saved your stingin' behind! I bet you didn't even say thank you!'

Wasp jerked forward. 'Well maybe—'

'Beetle. Wasp.' Weevil snapped.

Almost instantly, Beetle backed down. Wasp scoffed, turning her head away.

'What matters is that we're all ok,' Weevil said. 'And that we can all cross the stone stream together.'

Ant looked up. It was starting to get lighter. This little hiccup threw his plan off course but they could still make it to the stone stream before it got too dark if they kept moving forward.

'I knew Ant could take care of those spiders no problem.' Beetle danced around Ant as they walked on. 'I bet he showed them who was boss!'

'He didn't fight them.' Wasp moved to fly just above Ant. 'He sent them after some flies or something.'

Weevil stopped walking, stumbling as she turned to face Ant. 'You told them about the Bluebottles?'

Ant lowered his head and slowed to a stop. 'I didn't know what else to do. I wanted to save Wasp.'

'By sentencing others to their deaths?' Weevil planted her claws in the dry ground. 'You've just killed those Bluebottles!'

'They're just Bluebottles! Who cares! Ant saved the day *again*! So what if a few stupid little flies get eaten?' Beetle shuffled in front of Ant. 'What would've you done, huh?'

Ant pulled Beetle away from Weevil, stepping between them. 'I wasn't thinking. I just…'

He was a monster. A murderer. Those Bluebottles weren't doing anything to anyone. They were just living their lives and now they won't have lives to live! Ant looked between his friends then, in a heartbeat, he turned around and scurried back the way they had come.

Arriving at the stoat once again, never in his life did Ant think he'd be happy to see a swarm of Bluebottles. He left them undisturbed, occupied by the rotting flesh of the large creature as he searched for the spiders.

'Oh, are you kidding me?' The striped spider let out a frustrated sigh as it climbed down from the spindly branches of a dead shrub.

'We thought we had you.' The long-legged one was camouflaged amongst the dirt. 'Tunneller, he got out.'

The third spider emerged once again from under a precariously placed leaf.

'Wasp did too.' Ant said, attempting to seem valiant.

'So, why are you here?' The long-legged one got up from its resting spot, creeping towards Ant.

'Do you *want* to be eaten?' The striped one snickered.

'Are you here to gloat?' Tunneller hissed.

'What? No! No-' Ant tried to stand his ground. 'We're going to cross the stone stream tonight. I'm here to ask if you want to come with us.'

The spiders laughed in unison; it was excessive and condescending.

'Why would we go all that way?' The long-legged spider gestured to the nearby Bluebottles. 'We've got food right here.'

'Besides,' the striped spider added. 'The stone stream is ages away. We're not walking all that way because you invited us.'

'Crossing the stone stream is a death wish, little ant.' Tunneller crawled over to Ant, placing one of its front legs on him. 'Are you really willing to take that risk?'

Ant squirmed under the weight of Tunneller's claws. 'You guys said it yourself! Food is scarce!'

The three spiders looked at each other. Tunneller's leg pushed down harder on Ant's head.

'There's nothing here anymore!' Ant pleaded. 'Across the stone stream there's enough food for all three of you and then some!'

'I like the sound of that.' The striped spider leaned close to Ant, 'but how will you cross if we eat you right now?'

Tunneller lifted its leg. 'We'll follow you across the stone stream.' It said, dusting itself off.

'We will?' the other two asked in unison.

'*And*, if he doesn't fulfil his promise,' Tunneller dipped its head close to Ant's, 'we'll eat him.'

Ant scrambled to his feet and stumbled ahead a little, putting some distance between himself and the spiders. 'We need to get moving.'

Regrouping with the others, Ant didn't stop to explain what was happening.

'I can't believe you're bringing *spiders* with us.' Beetle whispered. 'You know none of them can be trusted.'

'It was either bring them or let those Bluebottles die.' Ant whispered back, ending the conversation there and then.

Ant's pace slowed to a purposeful crawl as they approached the edge of the heathland. The sound of the big boxes whizzing by made it hard to gauge if there were any nearby threats. The others stopped beside Ant, copying his careful movements.

'I don't see anything big and scary! We're so close I can almost taste all that food!' Beetle shouted, eager to continue forward which he did without a second thought.

Then Ant saw it — the outline of a bird perched on a nearby post.

'Beetle! Wait!' Ant shouted back, unprepared for the gravelly terrain he stumbled across. 'Beetle! There's a bird!'

Weak with hunger, he couldn't keep himself upright anymore. Each step forward would send him left or right instead. He was hopeless. Helpless. It was too late. The bird had spotted Beetle.

With wings spread, it looked almost beautiful. The light lit it up from behind and the air parted as it dove for Ant's friend.

It never reached him.

The bird pulled upwards, frantically flapping its wings at something.

'Wasp!' Ant barely managed to make it over to Beetle; his attention was focused on Wasp's every movement.

'What a silly little wasp.' Tunneller teased, standing just beside Ant.

'She saved my life.' Beetle watched in astonishment. 'She saved *my* life.'

It wasn't long until there were too many birds to count. The fight became one big mass of flapping wings and shrill screams of frustration.

The spiders quickly lost interest in the fight, talking about who-knows-what instead. Weevil and Beetle both turned to Ant, hoping that he'd have an escape plan.

'We should leave while they're distracted.' Weevil said softly.

The spiders perked up and wandered back over. 'Are we going?' The striped one asked.

'Not without Wasp.' Ant turned from the others.

In an act of betrayal, Ant heard Weevil discussing something with the spiders before the long-legged spider snatched him. 'Okay, buddy. Let's get going.' It said, fighting against Ant's escape attempts.

'But we can't leave Wasp!'

'We don't have any other choice! We're outnumbered, Ant!' Weevil attempted to shove Ant and the spider forward.

Beetle hurried back over to them. 'I think I found us a place to hide.'

Ant fought with everything. He had to try to free himself but the spider was stronger and quicker than him. It carried him with outstretched arms, practically shoving him into the small cave created by two large stones resting atop each other.

Against Ant's demands, the striped spider blocked up the only exit with a hastily spun web where it sat and stared.

'She's going to die!' Ant stood as tall as he could, attempting to push past Beetle and Weevil.

'She's probably already dead,' Tunneller said, an indifference in both his voice and his nonchalant demeanour.

'Not helping.' Weevil turned her back to the spider and focused on Ant. 'Wasp saved all of us. If you go out there now you could get yourself killed —'

'Yeah, and I don't want you to die; you're my friend!' Beetle nudged Ant.

'— and if you get killed, Wasp's sacrifice would've been for nothing.'

Turning his back on the others, Ant stared into the darkness. It mimicked his mind well. A shadow cast by rocks he felt trapped between.

A silence had the creatures in a chokehold. Not one of them dared to say anything lest another bird - or something bigger - was lurking nearby. Gripping this silence, however, was a claw of sadness. Even thinking about the other side without Wasp nearby felt wrong. Ant felt alone. Beetle argued that they hadn't known Wasp for that long so they didn't need to cry on her behalf but Ant knew he was lying to himself. Ant knew Beetle mourned her.

They passed the time in silence, each thinking about their loss. Darkness had etched across the sky when they ventured from the cave.

It didn't take long for them to reach the edge of the stone stream, although calling it a stone stream was an understatement.

'It's more like a stone river.' Weevil stepped away from the edge. 'I don't know if we can cross it.'

'Of course, we can cross it.' There was mock determination in Ant's voice. 'We *need* to cross it.'

'And how exactly do you intend to do that, little ant?' The spiders crept up to the edge themselves, peering across.

No big boxes were floating along it and as far as anyone could tell, there were no birds, but crossing it still posed many risks. Ant looked at the others. Wasp was the only one capable of flight.

'We'll just have to make a run for it.' Ant tried not to visualise the consequences of his statement. He may have saved those Bluebottles but he couldn't save his friends.

'I could get across there, easy.' Beetle half-boasted, putting two legs carefully onto the stone. 'I could take you on my back.' He looked up. 'One at a time, naturally.'

'That could work.' Ant turned to the spiders who shared sceptical glances with each other.

'We want proof.' The spiders stepped away from the edge.

'Weevil, you go across first.' Ant suggested. 'Then the spiders can decide if they want to come, too.'

Beetle climbed onto the stone stream; Weevil clung to him.

Each trip across the stream went smoothly, say for a few minor hiccups when the long-legged spider and Beetle got into a bit of a leg-tangle. Whilst Beetle appeared to be gaining confidence on the strange terrain, every return saw him growing wearier.

'Just you to go, Ant.' Beetle stood proudly next to his friend, his body clearly close to giving up.

'We can wait for a bit,' Ant suggested. 'You look exhausted.'

'Me? Exhausted? No way!' Beetle tabbed the ground. 'Besides, we should probably leave while it's still quiet.'

Ant didn't want to overwork his friend but Beetle made a compelling argument.

'Fair point.' Ant followed Beetle to the edge of the stone stream. 'I'll walk beside you, saves you having to carry me.'

'Fine by me, buddy!' Beetle set off with Ant in tow.

The stone stream was strange. It was flat but not smooth and it seemed to span a million paces either way with no end in sight. Beetle made it look easy but small grooves and little rocks made it difficult for Ant to walk in a straight line. He focused on the others ahead to keep himself from falling behind. They were his guiding light in the growing darkness.

Ant's focus was broken by Beetle who shoved him forward. Appearing in the distance were two bright eyes racing towards them.

Right there and then, Ant knew what it was like to be a rabbit struck with fear as a fox chased it through the grass. Beetle fell behind, the exhaustion finally catching up with him. Without hesitation, Ant doubled back, pushing Beetle forward.

The eyes of the big box were blinding as its head grew nearer. I had to have been a mere twenty paces away from them; there was no way they were going to make it. Ant closed his eyes and braced himself.

The past fifteen dawns had been difficult but Ant was proud he had never given up. Everyone had lost a lot, including friends and family and he was glad it had been that way until the very end. Every dawn had been a struggle and Ant was glad he could finally rest.

Nothing.

Opening his eyes, he realised that he was still alive. He watched as the big box retreated into the shadows, leaving him and his friend in one piece.

Frozen to the spot, Beetle stammered, trying to find something to say.

'You and me both.' Ant said, still haunted by the thoughts of his demise. He gently nudged his friend forward.

The big box aside, the final trip across the stone stream was easy enough, both arriving at the other side relatively unscathed. The spiders seemed uninterested in them, far more eager to hunt for food.

'Thank goodness you made it!' Weevil patted both of her friends but Ant didn't respond.

Something had caught Ant's attention. Something nearby. Something glowing red and orange.

If you are interested in finding out more about how you can help to support our delicate ecosystem, contact BUGLIFE - THE INVERTEBRATE CONSERVATION TRUST, SC-040004

A Guide to a Better Life
A.C. Brown

Valentine -
I couldn't remember anything when I had woken up on the edge of town, my clothes soaked through despite the lack of rain and some kid was kicking my foot. They scattered the moment I lifted my head and with quite a bit of effort, I got to my feet.

I hobbled a while through town, my legs feeling like they were made of pins and needles, where I eventually found my way to the animal rescue. I don't know why I went there other than it was the nearest place, aside from the pub, that still had the lights on.

The woman behind the counter had initially thought I was a drunk who had stumbled in but she stopped short of shouting me out of the building. Instead, her eyes grew wide as she slowly picked up the phone from its receiver while I unthinkingly sat down on one of the waiting room's couches, deaf to her whispering to the other person on the call.

I had been sitting there quietly for several minutes, staring blankly at the wall as the woman's gaze burned holes into the back of my head. Eventually, a police officer had burst into the room before he skidded to a halt and stared at me disbelievingly. The paramedic had to shove him out of the way to rush to my side and grabbed my chin to look me in the eye.

'The fae,' he tutted, pulling a cloth out of his pocket to wipe at my face. 'Can't immediately tell what they've done to him but the blood is likely his – on a technicality if he's a changeling. Either case, he's not undead.'

'Do you know him, miss?' the officer called to the woman, who mutely shook her head. 'Alright, well, we'll be taking him for now but we might need to stop by in the future – to jog his memory.'

I didn't resist the paramedic when he pulled me out of the chair, his hand tight round my wrist as he pressed his thumb against my pulse, where he led me to what looked like a hospital. Thinking back, it was really a clinic that was built on the edge of town and not all that far from where I had woken up, that likely only tended to people who had a run-in with the supernatural.

The paramedic took me to the back of the building, down a hall of doors where he sat me down on a bed. I don't remember anything after that – only the following morning.

When morning broke, with the world seeming far too bright, I felt like I had been scrubbed clean and despite the fact I ached all over, it didn't diminish my sense of relief. A nurse came in a few minutes later, greeting me with breakfast, my tongue stuck to the back of my throat. There was a giddiness to her, bubbling beneath the skin but she was patient as she helped me to eat and wiped my mouth. I had felt like a child in her presence, even though I couldn't remember what that was like, answering her simple questions that made me doubt my intelligence.

What colour is the sky? How many fingers am I holding up? Where are we? What day is it? What is your name?

The last three questions gave me a headache trying to answer. I had been gone a while, somewhere where time was strange before I woke to the kid by my feet. I could feel the giddiness drain from her with every unanswered question but the lack of a name seemed to make her genuinely concerned.

The name Celyn kept coming to the forefront of my mind but I knew it wasn't mine. Just as a frown graced her face, I had managed to spit out Valentine, red words that had stood out on a white poster as I had stumbled through the rescue's doors. The nurse simply raised a brow as she gathered the dishes and left the room, calling over her shoulder that a doctor would see me shortly.

While I waited for the doctor to arrive, I stared at the blank ceiling. Searching for my memories that I for some reason expected to be hidden behind a sort of wall or buried deep within a gilded chest. There wasn't anything there, as if they had been cut away like burnt hair.

Celyn -
When I had walked into that animal shelter I almost immediately turned around.

That couldn't have been Tyson, I told myself, *it must just be a look-alike.* But the scar travelling up the side of his face is what made me go to the front desk and ask about the man bottle feeding a kitten.

Tyson had been missing for several months. He'd been out on a job in the countryside, fae lands, he was the only one who didn't make it back. His boss was nonchalant over the phone when she'd told me that Tyson had disappeared. No trace of him left.

Of course, I immediately looked into where Tyson's job had taken him, to see if he'd had a violent outburst, as he tended to do and angered someone even his boss didn't want to deal with.

I also interrogated his fellow bodyguard; it was stupidly easy to abduct him with a young, pretty woman and a pill in his whiskey but he instantly wailed that he didn't know where my Tyson was and that the last he'd seen was when he went storming off into the woods.

So, against the "advice" of my colleagues I put up missing person posters despite the very likely possibility that he was dead. The fool wouldn't have noticed if he'd wandered through a fairy ring and started stomping on fae houses.

Even if he did, he thought that I'd been exaggerating when I'd told him just how dangerous they could be. He left the iron rings behind.

The man working at the animal shelter was nothing like him. He was quiet and patient while I gaped at him like a fish, a gryphon cub half-asleep on his foot. My Tyson didn't like being looked at and would glare at anyone who's gaze fell on him for a moment too long, even I wasn't allowed to admire him.

'Tyson?' I called, which suddenly made the man freeze, tilting his head as he turned the name over in his mind.

'It sounds... familiar but not right.'

What does that mean? I wanted to scream as I took a deep breath and held it for a few moments. The woman over the phone had said he'd seemed a little confused, a haze to his eyes when he'd walked in a few months ago. He'd been living at the rescue for all that time, being paid pennies to feed himself.

Despite being an info-broker, I couldn't find him - it was all dumb luck when I'd seen the rescue in the paper, my niece having been begging for a puppy for her twelfth birthday and the notice of the man who'd likely been taken by the fae.

'Well, what's your name now?'

'Valentine,' he said with a sheepish smile that showed the dimples that Tyson tried to hide. It almost made me miss what he'd said.

'Valentine?' The holiday that Tyson hated with a passion, a waste of money he said, a waste of time. I don't know if he'd laugh or groan at the irony.

'You can call me Val for short.'

'What do you remember before you ended up here?' I'd been told he remembered nothing but they'd only asked when he'd first shown up and apparently hadn't tried since then.

'Nothing, really,' he shrugged, absentmindedly stroking the cat pressed up against his thigh. 'Didn't have much on me 'fore you ask, just the clothes on my back.'

How badly did he piss off the fae? I wondered, swallowing back a sigh, *if his boss found out he'd lost everything, she'd dock double from his pay to replace it. Assuming she'd hire him again. He's much too soft now.*

Tyson had only been hired as that witch's bodyguard because he was an aggressive asshole who took everything the wrong way, the perfect man for a woman who'd angered just about everyone and their mother. This… *Valentine* had been patient enough to learn how to work with scared and feral animals - Tyson barely had the time for a plant.

'Who are you, anyway?' He said as he seemed to stare right past me, 'are you with the police? Already told you lot what I remember.'

'No, no.' I felt a shiver go down my spine. Perhaps it was for the best he'd lost everything if the police had come knocking – Tyson couldn't lie for shit.

'Ain't with the police,' I tried to smile, knowing a laugh would sound too forced. 'We're dating y'see, or well… maybe not anymore, but you went missing and I went looking. Didn't really think to look a town over from where you'd disappeared. Not customary of the fae.'

How the World was Made
Issy Thompson

the making of iron gall ink

not by a god or an explosion
but triggered by
a wasp
of the family Cynipidae
who's larva secrete chemicals
swelling the oak bud, so that the word
can dwell

whilst the larva mutates
and the husk of the word's potential is
gnawed through
by a flying thing, off to do it all again

then the word-that-could-be is a woody sphere
plucked from the branch and shoved deep in a pocket
along with pretty rocks, a used tissue
some keys, a dried flower

(the word is yet unformed
the word gestates
pocketbound
in the dark like an infant wasp
ready to do it all again)

remembered
only to be crushed into pieces
its tannic shell cracks beneath the pestle
its emptiness broken by the blow

the speechless one seeks out rust, scrapes
it from the hinge of their unused jaw, shakes
it all up in a jam jar
hoarse
stands still for a quarter moon

staring at the body of the word turning purplish-black
(bruise blossom, astringent truth)
until the scratching and scratching and scratching has to
begin

as the word is afflicted upon the page
and the speechless one wishes for the pestle:

hollowness gushes

the word is born.

If you or someone you know has been affected by any issues covered in this piece, please contact the BOOTSTOCK ASSOCIATION, SC-036225

Green Vitriol

Issy Thompson

A chemical name encompassing iron sulphates,
a key component in iron gall ink

ferrous sulphate hasn't got the same ring to it, but
vitriol,
green vitriol, now that's
caustic –
that's
corrosive –
(in conspiracy with the right chemical accomplice)

that's something that will eat the paper it's written on over
hundreds of years,
 self-destructing so sluggishly
we hardly see the paper slough.

imagine these words consuming themselves,
burning away the page, all because
bitterness blames, makes
beauty comes out in blotches
and the language is self-loathing – we are akin

imagine
(now I'm bold enough to tell you what to do)
imagine a gape in this page, the cellulose fibres
unthingmied
undid? uncoupled? untogethered?
from the form they once held –

what's the word for when
a thing is just erased, but
you know it must exist somewhere else,
in some other chemical form?

I suppose you could say
"change", but
the word I'm searching
for is laced with –

I was going to call change a spring word
an innocent word, but change has seen things,
change has been things. for one sweet syllable,
change has lived.

(let me breathe awhile, I do not know the name of
the chemical compound for bravery or love.)

I try to come up with an adage about the power of words;
their ability to burn.

like that time the class clown said I
smelled like a used tampon, but no, wait, that's
relevant,
because ferrous sulphate can be taken for anaemia,
and back then I was deficient,

and sometimes you need a little more iron in your blood:
a cutting edge to your words.

If you or someone you know has been affected by any issues covered in this piece, please contact the BOOTSTOCK ASSOCIATION, SC-036225

The Table
Scarlet Roe

'Come off it!' I whisper-shouted. 'Mr Swift, in The Flock?'

'I'm being dead serious,' Davey Greenfinch responded with such conviction. 'He was part of The Flock.'

If anyone was to look at Mr Swift, they would've thought he had been something like a leaf picker or a nest maker, not in The Flock. He was so small and scrawny, not to mention he had no sense of direction, always darting this way and that on his way home.

'Who told you that, then?' I pulled my gaze away from Mr Swift.

'My dad.' Davey shrugged. 'He knows Mr Swift quite well, apparently.'

'Yeah, right. Your dad says he knows everyone.'

Like me and my friend Davey Greenfinch, Mr Swift had been coming to The Table for years. He never really had much to do with anyone and didn't speak often but when you were able to rope him into a conversation, he spoke with great speed; I always struggled to understand him. Even though we didn't always talk to him, we all felt a profound loss when he stopped showing up. It felt, to me, like a feather had been plucked out of my wing. Something was missing and it was Mr Swift.

'He's probably found a new table.' Davey reasoned.

'Or he's dead.'

Davey gave me a weird look, but I could tell he was thinking it too. Mr Swift was older than us but not as old as Albert Starling, so maybe in his 50s or 60s at least. It wouldn't be out of the question to say that he died of old age, but he seemed well enough last time we saw him.

'Pah. He probably flew himself into one of those newfangled high-tech fences. The ones that zap you until you can't fly anymore,' Albert squawked. 'He never could tell which way was up and which was down. Though, this is rather a grim topic, don't you think?'

It *was* a grim topic but the thought of death seemed to be dancing around me as of late. It clouded my vision when I tried to remember the good times I've had at The Table and it made it really, *really* hard to think. Death first entered my life when mine and Davey's friend Molly House Martin stopped showing up. That was just as the tulips were beginning to bloom. After a few days, we figured we should go look for her. When we got to her nest, it was gone. Forcibly removed without a trace.

'Cats probably had her after she lost the nest.' Davey sighed.

The Table used to be full of life. Apparently, when it was first built they let all the bigger guys on. The Pigeons and a few of the Blackbirds. Even a couple of those Magpies. At least, that's what Albert told us.

'It got too crowded and the food was going to the ones that could have easily fetched themselves a few worms.' He huffed.

We only started coming after the string walls were put up. All sorts of characters were drawn to the food at The Table, back then. There was Ronnie Chaffinch and Amy Goldfinch. A personal favourite of ours was Willow Robin - she was a whole new kind of strange but she was nice enough. They all moved on, I suppose. I know Willow found herself a nice berry bush and all of a sudden; she was too good for us.

Now it was only me, Davey, Albert and the tulips that lined the edge of the grass.

We tried to keep our spirits high but it felt so empty with just the three of us.

'It's a sad sort of life, isn't it, my dear?' Albert lowered his head. 'All this empty air and no songs to fill it with.'

I didn't say anything. I didn't feel like it.

The tulips began to wither.

I hadn't seen Davey in weeks at this point. I don't know what happened to him and, quite frankly, I didn't want to know.

The tulips were now nothing but mush.

'It is what it is.' I bowed my head. I was the only one left at The Table.

If you or someone you know has been affected by any issues covered in this piece, please contact the BRITISH TRUST of ORNITHOLOGY, SC-039193

The Plastic Man
Issy Thompson

The plastic man was born of the earth, then changed. He was made of plants and trees and creatures and then the rocks piled high and his essence oozed under the weight. Then he was forgotten. Sediment gathered and the plastic man was buried. And there he stayed, until one day people dug him up. They discovered they could use him. He was malleable, they lived off his potential. They knew somewhere inside that they were depleting him, scuffing him down like the heel of a cheap pair of plimsoles but what did that matter? Everybody else is doing it, so why can't we?

That's what they told themselves.

The plastic man sat in the corner of the pub like he usually did and they all came like gannets after their workday, flocked to his corner and got him to buy them a round. They were a ferryman, a fencer, a forester, a freelance writer, a farmer, a furniture upholsterer and a found object artist. Getting the plastic man to buy a round was as simple as a clap on the back, a shake of the hand, a greeting, a grating chair being pushed back on the floor. Then the plastic man would rise whilst the younger ones flung themselves about the booth and shouted their orders over his shoulder.

The barmaid would make a half-hearted smile shape with her mouth and pull pints and pour drams; for the plastic man never spoke. He simply nodded behind him and then raised the glass of his own. Same again. And then he'd gesture to her, doing a swirly doodad with his finger: and one for yourself later. Then she'd tap an impatient foot in time with the radio whilst waiting for the head to go down and pull and pour and bash out an aggressive tab on the old-fashioned till before presenting him with the card reader.

Please tap here. And the plastic man would take out his crinkled leather wallet and extract with shaky fingers a clean plastic rectangle that made the machine go beep when he hovered it nearby.

One of them (the gannets) would rise, scooping the drinks together between splayed fingers and slosh their way back to the table, walking sideways like a dazed crab, dribbling beer on the carpet. Another one would follow to tip the barmaid and take the ritual lager plus nip and set it down in front of the plastic man, who'd be arranging himself back in his corner and squirreling away his wallet into the pocket of his filthy navy-blue duffle coat. His arrangements were sputters of movement from tremorous hands which buzzed with the same sound you felt from a pylon or one of those transformers surrounded by barbed wire with a sign that says danger of death. The others talked amongst themselves, occasionally elbowing the plastic man to enfold him in the conversation or inviting his weighted nod to give his side of an argument.

Time and again, the glasses would drain and the plastic man would rise and stagger across the warped wooden floorboards to the bar. At some point in the night, the ferryman would come to take the plastic man's arm, for guiding souls across the choppy sea was his second nature.

The night was over when the plastic man could rise no more. At that time, the fencer would wheel in his barrow that housed all his tools and the rest of the gannets would help manoeuvre the plastic man from his nook, coaxing him into the barrow to sit amongst the pliers and the post hole digger and the wire strainers. They usually made him sit on a carrier bag to protect his scrawny arse from the mud. Then the whole crew would exit the bar, followed lastly by the found object artist who'd be shoving their pockets full of soggy beer mats for their latest sculpture.

Up the wiggly streets, the gannet's procession swerved, with the plastic man in his barrow at the helm. One night, when the fencer and his barrow were absent, the farmer gave the plastic man a piggyback all the way up the hill; ended up with sick all down his shoulder.

The barrow was the most dignified option for all.

Under the starry street-lit muddlement of sky that exists over a rural, coastal town the procession would climb to the highest point, overlooking the bay, where the plastic man lived in his asbestos house. Nobody knew how such a frail soul got himself back down to the pub each day but each time the gannets burst through the pub doors fresh from the hell-that-is-work: there the plastic man would be. But for now, it was time to wheel the plastic man down the overgrown garden path and tip the barrow to the angle where the plastic man would be half standing and able to grab hold of the door handle. By that point he'd have sobered enough to go inside. They never went in with him: asbestos hung like crystals from the ceiling and rosettes of mould patterned the walls. If the plastic man made it into his bed or simply crumpled up on the hallway carpet they'd never know. Once the door was shut behind him, that was that. You might be anxious or afraid for him but let me tell you: once the door shuts, the plastic man disappears…

*

It was Tuesday and the furniture upholsterer was the first one to barrel through the swing doors of the pub and crash down at the plastic man's side.

'And how's you the day pal?' the furniture upholsterer clapped the plastic man on the knee. In turn, the plastic man raised his hand and blinked his watery eyes.

'Good, good. Been a fine one out there the day, lots of snow on the hills, did you see it?'

A nod.

'And there's me, trapped inside the new bistro, stapling pleather to plywood to make their new banquettes – Blasta Pasta, they're calling it. A Scottish-Italian fusion.'

A slantwise nod.

'Indeed. Stick a Gaelic word on the front and the tourists'll go nuts.'

Then, in came the fencer and the forester, arm in arm.

'Hello yous', the forester said. 'This one near blinded himself the day, have a look – '

And they all peered in to see a huge welt on the fencer's eyelid.

'Wire pinged back.' The fencer explained. The forester tutted and kissed it better.

The rest of the gannets trickled in one by one and seated themselves at the plastic man's table as they did every day after work. The freelance writer was the last to arrive, having been stuck at their desk writing content for the Blasta Pasta website with one hand and using a broom handle to fend off AIs with the other.

All was as it always was. The gannets watched on with beady eyes as the plastic man rose and scuffled to the bar. After the pints had been poured and the nip had been drawn from the optic, the plastic man extracted his battered wallet as usual. The barmaid held out the card reader looking over his shoulder at the found object artist. They saw her gaze and looked bashfully at the floor. She was so caught up in this that it took her a while to register that there'd been no beep from the reader. When her wrist got sore, she said to the plastic man to just pop his card in. He grunted and did so with hands so old and arthritic that they took an age to type the four magic digits in.

A beep sounded. The screen lit up: card declined.

'Have you got another card?'

He ground his head from side to side.

Meanwhile the gannets watched on with beaks agape. Their disbelief thawed enough to start fumbling for change in their respective pockets and bags. Looking around at each other for confidence, they rose with their fistfuls of silver coins and dumped them on the bar in small slagheaps of wealth. Sadie – for that was the barmaid's name – sucked air through her teeth and cursed the lot of them for making cashing up twice as hard. They had the audacity to tell her to keep the change. But amongst the silver coins, Sadie found a pair of silver earrings made from can tabs, wound around with wire and beads. She slid them off the counter and pocketed them, searching the room for the found object artist, who winked.

She listened to the group of gannets turn their bright chatter to the serious matter at hand: When does the pension come in, old timer? Is there enough on the meter? Will you keep warm this night?

The plastic man looked like his plastic card: empty, depleted. They all seemed to see who he really was for the first time: old. No family. Frail and unkempt.

Spent.

*

The hill seemed steeper that night. The moon was well hidden by a smirry veil of cloud and a damp chill permeated their delicate bones. It smacked more of a funeral procession than a group of good pals on the way back from the pub. Running through all their minds in the various ways thoughts form to each individual was the common theme of *What Do We Do with The Plastic Man?*

The ferryman phrased it to himself like this: a ship in distress – was there any hope in towing it to harbour for repairs or should it be abandoned to the sea? (assuming all human life had been evacuated of course). The farmer was wondering if the plastic man would even accept help if offered or stamp his feet like a stubborn heifer refusing to enter the barn.

The plastic man himself was quiet, as usual but that night his silence was not calm. None of the gannets could tell what he thought but those gnarled fingers worked away at the cuff of his jacket until the seam was unravelled and the button came off. All were quiet going down the garden path. At the doorstep, the plastic man rose, unaided and pushed open the unlocked door to reveal the gloomy hallway. The gannets looked at one another. Who would act? He was in and had about shut the door before the forester stuck out a steel toe-capped foot to stop it closing fully.

'Listen, can we just come in to check the lights work? Don't want you sitting there in the dark.'

Streetlamps illuminated the whites of the plastic man's eyes as he peeped his head round the door. Then his face receded. Then the door opened.

On the way in, the forester flipped the hallway light switch. Nothing. So, they all went in guided by the bluey light of their phones and congregated in the pitch black living room. The plastic man shuffled to an armchair with the stuffing falling out, sat down and closed his eyes.

The place stank of piss and mould. The found object artist pulled their bandanna up and over their mouth, gagging at the thought of all the spores now living rent-free in their lungs.

Then there was snoring. The plastic man was asleep with his head lolling to one side.

'He canny stay here,' stage-whispered the farmer. 'I'd no suffer my animals to live in this dump.'

'I mean, obviously,' agreed the fencer, and the rest of them nodded.

'But what do we do with him?'

*

They'd been drinking, so of course the most logical solution was to take him to the caves above town. Not the homeless shelter (too many instances of Narcan deployment) and not the police (a cell and questions that the plastic man wouldn't be able to answer) and to be frank they were all a bit scared to take him home to their respective sofas, so the caves it was.

Two of them stayed whilst the rest went off to their homes to gather supplies: A hot water bottle, a sleeping bag, a camping light, matches and kindling; some excess furniture foam as a bed and a couple of cans of soup to heat up in the flames; an old lifejacket as a pillow and some old oilskins in case it rained.

When they'd feng shui'd the cave into something resembling comfortable and got a fire burning nice and steady, it was time to retrieve the plastic man from his asbestos house and cart him up the path. So rocky and root gnarled it was that they had to stop and lift him and the barrow over tricky sections, all by phone-light. This carry-on lasted a lot longer than anticipated; the gannets were dishevelled and sweaty-pitted by the time they smelled the woodsmoke that signalled the end was near. The fire itself had faded like the gannets' surety that they were doing the right thing. There was a general lack of talking as the group emerged from the hazel brush and into the clearing at the mouth of the cave. Far below, the waves churned like stomachs in the dark recesses of the body.

'Here we are then.' The fencer set the barrow down. The words hung damp in the air.

The furniture upholsterer and farmer busied themselves with the dwindling fire, using a bit of copper pipe to blow on the flames, adding a bit of straw to the top. Braver and braver, the fire investigated each new twig it was fed, tentative at first but building up until it had the confidence to engulf whole logs. The smoke, puffy and thick from the moisture in the wood went up to the ceiling of the cave then flowed out and dispersed to the sky.

The plastic man sighed a big, long sigh and his chest cavity ached and rattled a bit as he exhaled. The icefloe inside was starting to move.

'Right then lads and ladies, thems and theys', announced the ferryman. 'Don't know about yous all but I've a boat leaving for Castlebay in about two hours. I'd best be off.' And it was true, the rosy-fingered dawn was starting to tear at the edges of the night sky. The rest of the gannets mumbled their excuses too and, one by one, they stopped to ruffle the plastic man's greasy hair and give him a wee pat on the shoulder as they filed away. The forester draped an old fleecy blanket over the plastic man's knees and the fencer got him to grip a nice hot cup of tea.

'You'll be just grand,' he whispered, crouching down to his eye level. 'We'll come see you after hell-that-is-work, we promise. You'll want for nothing.'

And there they left the plastic man.

*

Footsteps fading. Quiet chatter dispersing amongst the woods. Birdsong and exhalations and exchanges of gasses from plants and trees.

Light was returning. Colour was returning. Colour that the plastic man hadn't seen in millennia. So used was he to the dingy interior of the pub and the rotting shell of his asbestos house. For the sake of this story, we'll leave aside the usual pain and peril of alcohol withdrawal and just say that as the plastic man watched colour return to the earth, all the grey badness left his body. Each log he added to the fire burnt the disease from his liver and each plume of smoke that rose took with it the desire to drink until the malformed neural pathways of craving and abuse had uncoiled themselves like a fern in spring.

The plastic man felt himself return to his component parts. Gone was the extortion, gone was the extraction. He was no longer a commodity but a member of the community of plants and insects and trees.

Did he blame the gannets? The plastic man had been alive too long to do such things as blame. There had been gannets before those gannets - and other gannets before those. What mattered was that this set of greedy, beady eyed guzzlers had taken a step back and realised who they were and what they were doing and what drove them to do such a thing. For gannets nest on cliff's edges and don't exactly lead comfortable, stable lives. Imagine the cone-shaped egg is the earnings the gannets make from hell-that-is-work: how easy it is for it to roll off the ledge, or to be swiped by a predator of fate. Such a meagre speckled egg to begin with.

No, the plastic man didn't blame. The gannets flocked to him because his small plastic rectangle represented safety and stability.

When what they really needed to feel was the ground beneath their feet. The steadfastness of the earth.

'No,' the plastic man spoke into the morning air. 'No I don't blame those hungry gannets.'

He sighed again, and again it ached.

*

The day wore on. It was overcast but beautiful. Through the layer of cataract cloud, the sun shone overhead emitting a gentle warmth.

In the mouth of the cave, a wizened old man sat watching a tiny little fly crawl on his eyelashes. He looked through the branches to the sea, like a blue china plate, chipped white where the waves splashed, far away. There was space between his thoughts. He was noticing it now.

Space between each breath, a place to rest before his chest did what it was made to do and expanded again with air. Space up there in the sky amongst the frayed clouds and the seabirds.

*

The afternoon was over when the fencer, the forester, the furniture upholsterer, the farmer, the freelance writer, the ferryman and the found object artist met outside the pub and made their way up the rambling path to the cave above town.

'We should come up here more often,' suggested the found object artist, picking oak galls off branches to crush and mix with rusted nails. They would use them to make ink for writing love letters to Sadie.

'Sure, aye' went the gannets, and a load of happy nods.

*

There was nobody there when they entered the clearing. All that could be seen was a big lichen-covered stone sat in the mouth of the cave.

'He's done a runner.' The farmer shook his head.

'We should have checked in the pub,' went the forester.

'Or his manky house,' cut in the furniture upholsterer.

'No, look!' The fencer and the found object artist crept up towards the stone. It was so crusted in lichens and mosses that it looked like it had been there millennia. How had they missed it before? The shape of the stone was almost that of a face…

That wasn't lichen, that was a beard.

'He's here!'

The gannets flocked round. Some of them started to cry but didn't know if they were happy or sad or both. The plastic man was no longer a man. He was a living stone.

He was in the earth.

He was the chlorophyll in the leaves of the surrounding trees.

He was the wings of the dragonfly that alighted from a birch.

He was nowhere.

He was everywhere.

*

Picture a clearing and the mouth of a cave. Overlooked by a large, lichen-clad stone are a group of seven gannets and a barmaid sitting around a crackling fire. They're whittling branches, they're watching the clouds, they're writing songs, they're making art from leaves…

If you are interested in discovering more about how the BOOTSTOCK ASSOCIATION supports education for underprivileged children, please feel free to contact them directly, SC-036225

Mayhem
Anya Kimlin

WARNING: THIS PIECE CONTAINS LANGUAGE THAT SOME READERS MAY FIND OFFENSIVE

I'm a great big geek in a great big glass jar; the lid is on so tight it's suffocating me. Today's attempt to smash the jar proved that servants, comfortable beds and food make more effective bars than titanium.

My grandfather's voice runs through my head:

...embarrassment... barbaric brat... ugly monstrosity... mother-killing-brat... I smash my fist at full force into the stone wall. The pain stops the voice. A second blow breaks the skin on my knuckles. I lick the wound. The taste of my blood calms me and reminds me that I want to live.

My ribs send pain messages to my brain as I sit down at my desk to remove my sodden trousers. I fling them onto the school uniform mountain. The trousers cover up the fucking falcon on the front of an antiquated tunic. As the son of the king, when my clothes get dirty I order new ones instead of sending them to the laundry. I swing the chair until it faces the desk and shove aside the mugs and plates. Crisp packets rustle when I lay my head on my arms and close my eyes.

... clumsy oaf... barbaric monstrosity ... you'll never escape...I have eyes everywhere... I will hunt you down...

He's been dead three years but my grandfather's voice is still in my head. Whenever I shut my eyes it's worse because I can see him.

'Angus!'

I lift my head a little and turn it towards the door. 'Go away.'

Dad sounds pissed. I'm not in a state to deal with him. Why did I come back? When Matt said he was hungry, cold and he was going home, why didn't I tell him to fuck off.

The doorknob turns. 'Did I lock it?' I whisper. In case I didn't, I shove my copy of *Pride and Prejudice* into the bottom desk drawer.

The handle stops turning. I breathe out.

'Angus!' He bangs on the door.

'I'm doing my homework. I'll be out when I'm done.'

'You didn't go to school today. You have no homework.'

Using the desk for support, I stand up and limp over to the bed.

'Angus! Out. Now.' He punctuates it with thumps on the door. The door is nearly a thousand years old and was built to withstand armies. When my grandfather dragged me kicking and screaming out of the palace nursery, I chose a room in the original castle wing because of the fortifications.

'I'm naked.' With any luck the thought of seeing my pasty monstrosity without clothes will make him back off.

'Get dressed and come to my office in...' I imagine him standing there, immaculate in his uniform, tapping his polished boots on the cobblestone floor and checking the time on his BOB[2] wristband, '...five minutes.'

'You can fuck off,' I say so he can't hear me and stick a finger up in the general direction of the door. We both need to cool off before we meet. It goes quiet. I use one of the bedposts to lower myself onto the mattress. I lie down and stare up at the canopy. After a rest and a shower, I'll go and find him. We can kiss and make up.

'BOB.' I activate the palace's cloud-based operating system.

'You called,' he replies in a disinterested tone. I've ring-fenced BOB's behaviour, just within my room, to treat me with disrespect. I've also given him a new voice. The original voice is rumoured to be my mother's. I have never heard her speak so I don't know if that is true or not. Outside of my room people bow, scrape, turn their backs to me, avoid my gaze and when they do talk to me, they call me Your Highness. I don't suit the term. BOB is one of my few true friends.

'Do you actually want something? Or are you just abusing my name?'

I ask, 'Play The Skuas - *Democracy Warriors*. The whole album. Start with *Shit Bomb the King*.' The title makes me laugh. It's about a flock of birds attacking my grandfather and killing him; they go on to eat his flesh and crap on his supporters. The group has been going since my grandfather was on the throne. If he had caught them, they'd have been executed. They are the only people the media appear to hate more than me.

'Yes, you balding monstrosity of a mortal,' he responds.

One day I will program him to sound less like a middle-aged man with his insults. 'That's the one thing I am not.'

'Monstrosity?'

'That was my grandparents' name for me.'

'Mortal?'

'I'm a mortal monstrosity but I'm not balding.' When I run my hand through my thick hair, it gets caught in the knots.

There's a pause. I can't have quiet or my grandfather's voice will start up again. 'BOB.'

'Whatever - do you want the music?'

'Yeah. Blast it.'

The bass starts and I close my eyes. It's a relief as the one from this morning's fight is struggling to see properly. For a few minutes I listen to Danny Wren's alto voice sing and scream about ending the monarchy. I imagine her coming to rescue me from this room. I focus on her taking the palace and use the music to block out my grandfather's voice. I've never seen her face because she always wears a mask.

A cold breeze disturbs my thoughts and raises my adrenaline. *Where did it come from?*

'Angus! I said my office in five minutes. It's now twenty minutes and thirty seconds. BOB turn that bloody awful noise off.'

He sounds like he is in my room but I didn't hear the door. The hinges have needed an oil for around a decade. I try to open my eyes, but they are swollen shut.

'I only recognise my Lord and Master.'

At least BOB didn't swear at him. He can be a little unpredictable. My sore eye is encrusted with gunk. With my fingers, I peel it open, wincing as I feel my eyelashes rip apart. The light makes me blink them closed before the fog clears.

'Passcode: 01010000 01100001 01110000 01100001, I am *the* Lord and Master. Turn that poor excuse for music off,' Dad says.

This time with effort, I peel my eyes open without my hands. It's still blurry but there is a figure dressed in green by the balcony doors. That's where Dad's voice is coming from. A gust of wind causes the curtains to sway.

'Yes, Your Majesty.' BOB reverts to using a robotic version of my mother's voice.

There are leaves in Dad's normally immaculate hair and his tunic is dusty. The cuff of the undershirt is torn. He shakes his head and brushes himself down. The black beady eye of the fucking falcon on Dad's chest fixes on me. If Dad hadn't been present, I'd have greeted it with a two-finger salute. Dad stands at the ready, watching me and waiting for me to speak.

'I'm not six anymore. I'm not confessing to anything you don't already know about.' I roll to my side, holding my ribs. 'What *do* you know?'

He moves forward and takes a strong grip of my elbow to help me to standing. 'Get in position. You are in disgrace.' He steps back onto last week's clothes pile. There's a loud plastic crack. He kicks the clothes and whatever he just destroyed out of his way. 'How did you get injured?'

I rub my arm where he had grabbed it. 'I threw the first punch.'

I can't actually remember who started it. If I tell Dad anything else then he might arrest Jack. Sometimes Jack starts it. Sometimes I do. It's not something he should be imprisoned over.

'BOB,' Dad barks an order at the digital system.

'Yes, Papa Smuffles?' BOB is back with his male voice and sarcasm.

Dad hasn't been in my room for about two years and nobody else will come in because of the mess. When I ring-fenced BOB, I hadn't specified he was only to be rude to me.

'It's Your Majesty,' Dad tells him in an even tone that gives nothing away. 'Locate Sir Gilbert. Inform him that His Highness, Prince Angus, requires medical attention but he's to finish sorting out the conference accommodation first.'

BOB makes a noise that is close to a *thunk* in response.

'I don't need a doctor,' I say, looking down at my feet. My first three toes are the same length and I have patch of hair at the base of my big toe.

His voice softens, 'That eye is concerning me. It will be looked at. Do you need to sit down?' Before I can object, he steps forward and takes my elbow again. Dad's grip is firm but more gentle as he guides me to sitting. He looks around the room, clicking his tongue on the roof of his mouth. After going through the empty drawers in a chest, he starts disturbing my piles of clothes. 'When was the last time you had a cleaner in here?'

'Bout two years.' My chest tightens and I need to breathe out the fear. There's no way I will get to keep my room this way. The mess is as much of a defence as the door; nobody else wants to come in here. I bite down on my cheek until I taste blood. It stops me from losing it as he touches my things. I'm several inches taller than Dad, but he's an accomplished soldier and he'd have me flat on my back before I could land a punch.

'What is this?' His face contorts in disgust as he picks up a plate with mould on it; its contents have long since been forgotten. 'It's ready to walk itself back to the kitchen. Is this why the kitchen is always sending request forms for new crockery?'

Dad picks up my school t-shirt, keeping it at arm's length and holding it between his thumb and forefinger; an egg stain covers the eye of the falcon on the front. 'This looks like the cleanest.' Dad throws it over to me. He picks up an upended chair, removes some chewing gum from the seat and, with an elegance at odds with the mess in my bedroom, he swings it round so he can sit on it backwards.

'Ach.' When I pull it on over my head, the t-shirt catches on my split lip and makes it bleed. I suck on it, tasting the salty, tangy blood. When grandfather beat me, if I could taste my blood, I knew I was still alive.

From his tunic pocket, Dad takes his precisely folded handkerchief. 'Now we need to deal with today.' He hands his handkerchief to me. 'You can't keep doing this, son. I assign you some of my best warriors to keep you safe. Where did you go?'

In the corner of the brilliant white square, another falcon accuses me. In my mind, they always find me guilty. I fold it and hold it tight against my lip to staunch the blood. I look at him but don't say anything. The one thing we do together is play BOB chess and just sometimes I place the king in checkmate. That's not going to happen today but I will settle for a couple of stalemates before I lay down and accept punishment. Until I work out what kind of bird my cousin sang like, I'm not dropping myself in it.

Faster than a falcon in a dive, Dad grabs my chin, positions my face so I can't avoid his gaze and he glares at me like a bird eyeing up his prey. The media reports that Dad is meek and mild but he's strong and agile. 'Where did you go? Answer me.'

'That hurts.' My attempts to pull away from him are unsuccessful and a bruise is forming on my chin to join the bruised ribs, split lip, and black eye. 'Dad, please. It's sore.'

'If I listened to your Uncle Tom and the rest of the country, right now, you'd be in a lot more pain.' He doesn't let go but his voice softens. 'We both know any form of corporal punishment I bestow would be useless. You've survived worse than I could dish out.' He releases my chin to turn back to BOB's base; Dad might be the system's chief architect but like most old people he still thinks he needs to look at BOB to talk to him. 'BOB! Remember who you are addressing.'

'Yes, my Lord and Master.' BOB's tone is sarcastic.

'That's an improvement. This morning's cartoon by Drawembad, please.'

'No.' I look away. 'You can't make me.'

...you're clumsy... you're ugly... you're too big... you took your mother from us... you can't get anything right... Grandfather screams in my head. I suck on my cheek and wince as I bite it to get a little more blood.

'I won't look.' Drawembad can't even put his real name to his work but, along with the other sewage workers at the Covesea International News (CIN), he has made it his life's work to ensure twenty million people hate me. I know it works because his cartoons made me hate myself. 'No. No. No!'

'Angus, I don't have your luxury of ignoring this.' Dad guides my chin, so I am facing forward but I refuse to open my eyes. 'The consequences of your behaviour have serious real-world implications. The new trade negotiations are important to the lives of every Islander.'

'All of them hate me. Why should I care about them?' The thought of opening my eyes and seeing what BOB is projecting, makes my chest hurt.

'Don't be ridiculous. They don't all hate you. You should care because...'

'...because...' I do a silly voice. 'I'm a prince and I have a duty to care for the people of Covesea Island because they are why I am so fortunate and can live in the Palace. I don't want to live in this prison and be the son of the fucking king.'

'I need you to do a press conference.' His voice is quiet, practically a whisper. For the first time ever, he ignores my swearing.

'I bet Matt doesn't have to face a press conference. Uncle Tom will just give him a whipping and ground him when...' I stop before I tell him where we went.

'Matt's not the king's son. You are. You will read out an official apology to the nation. Too many lives depend on me being seen to have you under control.'

'I need to vomit.'

There's a clank. Dad says, 'I emptied the bin onto the floor. It was overflowing anyway. If you need vomit or pee, use it.' He moves away again. 'You're not moving from that spot until you look at Drawembad's latest offering.'

'No. I won't. You can't make me.' I haven't seen a newspaper or watched any news since my grandfather died. I barely watch TV or check out BOBvid in case I'm on there. 'What if I need a shit?'

'Do you?'

'No but we're going to be here a long time. Figured we should be prepared.'

'I'll march you there and come in with you and march you back. Where's your tablet?'

'That's disgusting.'

'Can't say the idea thrills me either.' A drawer opens. *Where did I put Pride and Prejudice?* He can't find that. It forces my eye open. 'Top drawer of the desk.'

I open my eye. 'Dad... I can't see.'

'Breathe and remind yourself to only look out of your right.' I hear him open a drawer. 'Angus, calm down. Your eye is adjusting to not being able to see.' I feel him sit next to me. He touches my shoulder.

'How do you know?'

'When I was a teenager, my mother had a thing for removing the eyes of criminals. You're not the first one-eyed man in my life.' He rubs my back, calming me and I do as he tells me. 'Now close your good eye and open it again.'

I can see but I can no longer avoid the cartoon. On BOB's base is a 3D image that I guess is supposed to be me; it's dressed in a leather kilt with feathers. The nose is bulbous, the face grotesque but the sheer size and long greasy blond hair is so accurate. It's obvious who it is meant to be. At my feet, my father is kneeling. He quivers as I raise a barbarian's club over my head. The caption reads: *How can the King Laurence II negotiate with his enemies when he can't control The Royal Oaf.*

'Shows you what he knows. I don't squint anymore. I haven't for years,' I yell at Dad. 'BOB, turn that thing off.'

'You do not have permission to do that.' BOB's voice is my mother's again.

'What have you done?' Tears are stinging at the back of my eye, making the bad one burn. 'Dad, please. Turn that off. You know I can't do this. Dad?'

He places a hand on my shoulder. 'I'm sorry you had to see that. BOB switch off Drawembad. Add him to the restricted list.' My father squeezes my shoulder. 'I'm impressed with the work you've done infiltrating BOB.' He pats my shoulder before wandering over to the balcony doors and staring out to sea. He pulls the curtains back and opens the doors completely. 'Your honey pot is impressive. Until BOB spoke to me, I did not realise that you had ring-fenced him and changed him into an unrecognisable unit. But you forgot one thing.'

'I didn't forget anything.' My mind runs through my programs. 'I really didn't. I made myself system administrator and removed you.'

'You forgot Professor Weeks and I designed the system. When I gave BOB my passcode, he acknowledged me as *the*

Lord and Master - or his father. That pass code gives me control of all BOB's systems at all times.' He does a military turn. There's a triumphant smile on his face. 'I've returned your BOB base to factory settings and severely limited your access. You have school, the kitchen, a few educational sites, and an emergency line to security.' He winks at me. 'I'm sure you'll be able to get around it but it should take you a few days to get it back. The Skuas have been restricted permanently. Their influence on you is unwholesome.'

'No, it isn't.'

'How do you think it looks when lyrics like *bomb the palace* and *fuck the king* are blasting from *my* son's bedroom?'

'Do I have to do the press conference?'

'Yes and I'm confining you to your room under heavy guard until the end of the negotiations. That should be about three weeks. Professor Gordon has agreed to send you work to keep you busy and either Soc or I will take you out for exercise once a day.'

'I'm under house arrest?' There's no way I'm submitting to that. I'll find a way to get rid of my guards. Maybe next time I will escape down the Lang River and never come home.

'It's for your own safety.'

'You couldn't possibly put me before twenty million others. Just once.'

'Angus, that's never true.' His face becomes unreadable but I think his eyes are watering. 'I am trying to keep us safe. You're not a small child. You should understand that by now.' He's holding his fists. He is holding back. I'm doing the same so as not to lash out.

'There're the twenty million people that you give everything to and then there's Angus who you don't give a fuck about.'

'Language. Grow up, young man. You're seventeen now. Old enough to understand.' His knuckles whiten as his grip on his fist tightens.

A knock at the door prevents the argument from escalating. Dad goes to the door. 'Who goes there?'

'Sir Gilbert, Your Majesty.'

Dad unlocks the door and lets him in.

With military precision, Sir Gilbert enters. Holding a tray, he kneels in front of my father and bows his head. 'Your Majesty.'

I don't often get to interact with my father's friend and valet. Sir Gilbert fascinates me as he's one of the few non-Islanders to be allowed in the Royal Quarter. His short, grey hair blends into his light ash-grey skin.

My father says, 'See to Prince Angus's eye and other injuries. He's been fighting again. And get this room sterilised. It stinks. It can't be healthy.' He laughs. 'There are experiments on those plates that are almost ready to rise up against us. The last thing we need right now is a new enemy.'

'Maybe we could get His Highness to negotiate them onto our side. They might be more loyal than the current Soaring Warriors.' Sir Gilbert walks over to me and peers closely at me. There isn't a speck of dust on his glasses. I've never looked into his eyes before, they're a mother pearl. 'That eye needs greater medical knowledge than I have. May I call in an ophthalmologist, Your Majesty?'

I look away.

'Angus, look at Sir Gilbert until he says he's finished.' My father grabs my chin and guides my face back into position. 'Sir Gilbert, you have permission to do whatever you need to make my son and his room presentable. I am sorry to have to ask but can you stay late and make sure he doesn't leave this room tonight?' He lets go and stands back.

Adrenaline pushes me to stand without any help and I knock Sir Gilbert out of the way. I tower over my father, ready to beat him into compliance.

'You can't do that - it's Soc's birthday. I'm taking Bea. She'll kill me. You can't. House arrest has to start tomorrow.'

He squares up to me. It deflates me and when he takes my elbow, guiding me back to sitting, his expression is icy. 'Angus, you have proven today that you cannot be trusted to behave. All the dignitaries from the negotiations will be on that yacht tonight. You will not be allowed within a hundred metres of them.'

'Dad, no. Come on. I will behave. You can't do this to Soc?'

My father looks at Sir Gilbert who has positioned himself facing the wall. 'We are not alone. Remember your etiquette, young man.' The expression that he turns on me this time is that of king and not my dad. 'The crown prince had to leave work to be interrogated about you and then join in the search. *You* gave no thought to him then.' He stretches his arm out. 'Half the Soaring Warriors were out looking for you.'

'Your Majesty, please?' I forget about protocol and this time I try pleading with him. 'What about Bea?'

'You'll have to deal with her wrath. I'm quite sure that beautiful young lady will find an alternative date for this evening. Sir Gilbert, step forward. Have you finished with him?'

He obeys my father's command. 'May I get Your Majesty's help to lay His Highness back on the bed. I need to check his ribs.' Dad kneels on the bed so they can take hold of me, giving me no option for escape. They lie me down. My father pins my arms down and Sir Gilbert lifts my t-shirt.

I hold tight, only the duvet to stop me from pulling away from them. It's how I used to stay in place for one of grandfather's beatings. I suck on my cheek.

Sir Gilbert is professional as his cold hands feel my ribs. My hand grips more of the duvet and I remind myself that both Sir Gilbert and I are under my father's official orders. It helps me fight my nature and submit to what they are doing.

I find a new place to bite on my cheek.

'Well?' My father asks him.

'Just bruised. Do I have permission to medicate the prince?' I'm laid there with my chest exposed whilst they talk about me. My father has made it quite clear that we're under full court rules so I cannot object or even speak without being spoken to. When I try to straighten my shirt, my father slaps my hand away.

'If I say no, just how much pain will he be in? I'm tempted to let him feel the full consequences of this fight?' My father lets go of my arms and walks over to the desk. He moves papers and mugs out of the way, turns round to face us and leans back on it.

Sir Gilbert pulls down my T-shirt and he stands so he is facing my father but not looking directly at his king. 'He will survive without painkillers. We could go with a cream to help a little?'

'I know he won't use that unless you apply it and that would mean you staying overnight. It's your wife's birthday. Is there a suppository that would do the job?'

That makes Sir Gilbert look uncomfortable. I'm fighting to keep control of my anger and my father's teasing isn't helping. Sir Gilbert lays a hand on my forehead. 'I'm worried he has an infection. He might need antibiotics.' His hand moves to my shoulder, and he applies a firm pressure. It's like he knows I am fighting the urge to fight.

'You have my permission for any medication you think he should have. I trust you to find that balance between not going too easy on him and not torturing him.' He pats Sir Gilbert on the shoulder, in a rare moment of affection with a servant. 'If my son gives you any trouble, you're to use the Soaring Warriors to ensure his compliance. Do you understand, Your Highness?'

'Would it change anything if I said no?' I say.

'Not a thing. Under no circumstances are you to leave this room until I order otherwise. Goodnight, Your Highness.' Without another word or even a glance in my direction, my father leaves me alone with Sir Gilbert. [*To Be Continued…*]

Feathers
Sophie Martin-Lloyd

There was dust everywhere. She could see it along the countertops and the handle for the fridge. Giant dust-bunnies that whispered along the linoleum when she opened a door, unable to catch on the slippery floor of the apartment. It didn't matter how many times she swept and mopped and brushed and polished, the dust was there to stay - and often returned with a *vengeance.*

Rachel had always thought herself to be organised. A woman of refinement. She could remember being a little girl having tea parties with her dolls, just like they did in books and on television, and dressing up and curling her hair with rollers. There was a picture in her dad's wallet before he died of Rachel at ballet class, doing a perfect pirouette. 'That's my daughter,' he'd boast to his colleagues. 'She just got full marks on her maths test! We're very proud of our little lady.'

What he didn't tell his colleagues was how that little lady froze in the face of finger-painting and grass stains. Her proficiency in ballet wasn't because she was talented but because of how afraid she was of getting it wrong and falling on the dirty floor of the ballet studio. Rachel, Rachel, Rachel - so afraid of mess that she'd cry during a power-cut because she can't vacuum the stairs.

For most people, the natural mess of daily living was nothing to be concerned by. Rachel wanted to be one of those people for a long time. She wanted it so badly that she pretended it was fine and she pretended hard enough that she forgot what she was afraid of. But that didn't mean the anxiety faded.

Watching Jocelyn snooze at the dinner table, Rachel leaned back in her chair, listening to the dangerous *creak* of the metal legs bending under her weight. Jocelyn hadn't touched her plate. Surely the food had gone cold, her peas cold and disgusting, chips soggy and bland...

Rachel itched to throw it away.

No, she reminded herself, stalling any urges to reach out and grab the dish. Jocelyn needed to eat after a hard day's work. She tugged at her ponytail, twitching at the sharper-than-usual tugging.

To distract herself, Rachel inspected the laundry, watching the timer tick down from ten minutes to three. Her attention was caught because it had to be.

(Who knew what she would do if Jocelyn didn't get rid of her plate?)

The damp laundry caused her skin to crawl when she grabbed it, the wet cotton of t-shirts and heavy denim of jeans that Jocelyn had accidentally left between the washing machine and the wall creating a ripple effect down her whole body. Rachel shuddered in revulsion.

'No, no, no, no-' Even when she dropped them, however, the feelings remained. She wiped her hands frantically against her thighs, able to deal with the cold, damp sensation on her legs, if only her hands were decontaminated. More water wouldn't wash it away-

But now her legs were contaminated. *No. No, no, NO.* **NO.**

'Joss! JOSS!' Rachel screamed, breathing heavy. She tried to air-dry her hands, waving them manically in an attempt to make the damp feeling dissipate. It barely worked. And now her legs were wet and the sensations would sink into her like acid, and it would infect her bones until she wanted to cut them off, like a wayward butcher.

Where was Jocelyn? Why wasn't she helping. 'JOSS!' She sobbed, hearing the faint patter of water on glass. Rachel whimpered because Jocelyn had the *worst* timing.

To make matters worse, the damp clothes were now half-pulled from the machine, one jean leg flopping onto the dirty tile, a sock pushing her over the edge as it fell from inside the drum itself.

'Joss,' Rachel whined to herself, knowing Jocelyn couldn't hear. She couldn't storm in on her while she was in the shower. She'd been working all day in a hot, smelly kitchen and *no, what if she left her food out?* But she wouldn't have. She had her Health & Hygiene, she would have put any food she didn't eat in the bin…

Rachel squeezed her eyes shut as her mind tried to convince her otherwise. She trusted Jocelyn. She *loved* her and trusted her not to do something like that. They had talked about it. Rachel needed things kept clean or she would have breakdowns like this.

'I trust Joss.'

She trusted Jocelyn.

'I trust Joss.'

Her girlfriend wouldn't deliberately go out of her way to trigger her.

'I trust Joss.'

And even if she did forget, that was allowed. She paid their bills and worked really hard to support them both. If she'd forgotten then Rachel would clean up instead, and that would be okay. She cooked dinner! They didn't have a rule about one person doing the cooking and the other washing dishes - those things just fell to whoever got there first!

Breathing in deeply, Rachel nearly gagged on the smell of soap and mildew but forced herself to do it again. In and out. In and out. The smells eventually became background chatter, white noise to the patter of rain. Her legs were fine. The clothes from the washing machine had been cleaned with her favourite powdered soap and softener, and even if she did get debris on her legs, it was the *clean* kind. She had no reason to panic.

Opening eyes she hadn't even realised she'd closed, the young woman made a beeline to the kitchen. As she feared, Jocelyn had left out her plate but Rachel was there. She cleaned it up. The leftovers went in a box for Rachel's lunch tomorrow, and the plate deftly scrubbed in the sink. She used a disinfectant spray on the table, one that smelt like lavender and then her kitchen was returned to its usual pristine condition.

More present than before, Rachel noticed the open door for the bathroom and then the closed one leading into Jocelyn's space. 'Goodnight!' she called out, keeping all her previous panic out of her voice. 'I love you!'

Craning her ear, Rachel swore she heard a muffled noise and smiled to herself, biting her lip. She'd sleep in her own room tonight. If Jocelyn wanted some alone time, then that was fine - that was exactly why they had separate rooms!

'I love you,' she said to the closed door, pressing her fingers to her lips and then to the cool doorframe. 'See you tomorrow.'

After that little goodnight, she walked away, heading back to the laundry. She wasn't one to leave tasks undone. Bedtime could wait.

(She'd freak out later.)

-

The weeks passed sleepily that summer, the heat and summer showers sending Rachel into a tizzy. Her hair became unmanageable and Jocelyn was too exhausted from work to help her detangle the back strands.

'I might have to cut it,' she told her, laying face-down on the sofa. Jocelyn was idly watching the news, occasionally humming along to whatever earworm Rachel infected her with. 'Will you love me, even if I'm bald?'

Jocelyn grunted. 'I was bald.'

'Yeah - but you were the *hot* kind of bald,' argued Rachel, wincing when her scalp started to itch. She patted it warily, trying to avoid getting her nails caught in the rats' nest that was her head. 'I've seen pictures.'

'No, you haven't.'

Rachel frowned. 'I have.' Her frown only deepened as Jocelyn turned her head, looking back at her with her serious face on. Something about it disturbed her.

'No, Ray, you've not. You might believe you have, but you haven't.'

'Stop gaslighting me — I've definitely seen pictures. See, I'll get them.' To prove her point, Rachel grabbed her phone from the coffee table, unlocking it to access her apps. She felt Jocelyn's gaze on her like an iron poker as she accessed Jocelyn's profile, getting irked when she didn't recognise the woman in the pictures.

'Ugh, someone hacked your account or stole your name. Where *are* you?' Rachel clicked through the woman's pictures anyway, more sure that her girlfriend had been hacked as she scrolled through her memories and found previous profile pictures - the ones Rachel had picked of them together, cheek to cheek and oftentimes, lips to lips. She smiled at a Pride picture of them both with rainbow headbands and lesbian flags pinned to their bra straps.

'Rachel, you're ignoring what's in front of you.'

'Shh, look at us,' she cooed instead, showing Jocelyn the pictures. It didn't do anything to break her serious gaze and it made her angry. Really angry. 'We're fucking gorgeous and in love and you're not even looking! *Look at us,* Joss!'

Jocelyn stared into her eyes. 'You aren't listening.'

'You're the one not listening,' Rachel snarled, and she *hated* Jocelyn in that moment, wanted her to shut up and feel the agony she felt all the time.

She reached out to grab her chin but Jocelyn avoided her. When Rachel tried again, Jocely scrambled back. 'Stop moving!'

'Stop trying to touch me.'

'You're *my* girlfriend. *Mine.*' Rachel didn't understand why she said that but it felt wrong, the words dragging out of her mouth like sandpaper. She lurched off the sofa, legs tangling with blankets and a duvet - when had that gotten there? — except when she looked up, Jocelyn was gone. She heard a slam.

Her room.

'Joss! Don't hide from me!' Rachel got to her feet, stamping her foot. There were only so many places you could hide in a two-bed apartment.

She got *incredibly* lucky to run into Jocelyn in the bathroom door though, rather than either of their rooms.

'Rachel,' Jocelyn said, brown eyes wide and hurt.

Got you.

Like a viper, Rachel grabbed her arm and held her there, palm like lava as she held her girlfriend in place. 'Stop running away from me,' she demanded, all the hurt in her chest bubbling up into a whine. 'Please, Joss. I don't understand.'

Jocelyn's eyes somehow got wider, disbelieving. 'You're hur-'

'I know it's been difficult because of lockdown and - and work being stressful,' Rachel tried, desperate beyond belief. What if Jocelyn left her? What if Jocelyn decided she was worthless as a partner, or worse — as a *person*? Rachel didn't know if she could live with that kind of judgement.

Woozy at the thought, Rachel looked down at her hand on Jocelyn's arm. It looked wrong. She shouldn't be holding her like that, should she? No. No, she shouldn't. Rachel carefully peeled her fingers away, watching a red handprint bloom on her girlfriend's bare wrist.

'Oh. I did that.' Rachel stepped back in a daze, bumping up against the wall. Jocelyn faded from her vision which tunnelled at the realisation of what she'd done to her. She'd hurt Joss.

Like at the washing machine, time passed slowly. It turned syrupy and thick. Rachel's hand burned, her brain revolting at the idea that *her hand* caused that mark on Jocelyn's skin.

She fumbled for her phone, unlocking it again to search up a number. Any number. She needed help - she needed someone to tell her if she was in trouble.

There was a click. 'Police,' said Rachel, only half-listening to what they said next. 'I hurt someone. My girlfriend. She's hurt.'

Her lips moved but she didn't *feel* the words as she said them. They asked for Jocelyn's full name. Rachel's name. Rachel's address. Something about being in danger, or - or Joss being in danger?

'No! No, it was an accident, I've never done anything like that before.' Rachel hurried to add, 'She's not here anymore. I think she's gone.'

'Gone?' The operator's concern hit her like a tonne of bricks and Rachel staggered to her feet in an instant, just to check.

'I'll look! I don't know if she's here. Maybe she's just in her room?'

Rachel felt dizzy again as the operator spoke, phone pressed to her ear. Jocelyn - Jocelyn had to be in her room, right? She would have heard the front door unlock. A glance down the corridor showed the entrance closed and locked up tight.

Jocelyn's room.

She won't mind if I check, Rachel assured herself before turning the knob. The sight that greeted her was unprecedented - the bed stripped and the wardrobes empty. All of Jocelyn's decorations were gone, including her favourite green lamp and the photograph of Jocelyn with her foster-mum, Louise, when they went to Thailand for her eighteenth.

'She's not here,' Rachel told the operator, dropping to her knees. Her burning hand pressed against the grey carpet, stinging like a *bitch.* When Rachel looked down to see what she'd touched, all she saw was red, in the shape of her own handprint. 'Oh. She was never here.'

It came in flickers. Flashes. Jocelyn's distraught face and her words: *I deserve my anger. It's mine.*

Rachel looked down at her burned and weeping hand, from where she'd grabbed the bathroom radiator, and told the operator weakly, 'I need help. I think… I think I hurt myself. I'm burned. Help me. Please.' Her eyes stung, tears rolling down her cheeks. 'It *hurts*.'

'Officers will be at your location shortly. We'll try and get in contact with your partner. Just sit tight, Rachel. Whatever is happening there, we'll figure it out.'

'I want Joss,' she begged, pleaded. 'Please, I need her, I don't know how to do this without her.'

And in the next moment, it was almost like she *was* there, kneeling in front of her with those beautiful brown eyes. 'I'm here, Ray,' she promised. 'Hang in there. I'll always be here when you need me. Love you.'

Despite herself, Rachel smiled back.

'Love you.'

If you or someone you know has been affected by any issues covered in this piece, please contact SCOTTISH ACTION FOR MENTAL HEALTH. SC-008897 and/or RESPECT, SC-051284

Printed in Great Britain
by Amazon